There are a number of HORIZON CARAVEL BOOKS published each year. Titles now available are:

THE SEARCH FOR KING ARTHUR
CONSTANTINOPLE, CITY ON THE GOLDEN HORN
LORENZO DE' MEDICI AND THE RENAISSANCE
MASTER BUILDERS OF THE MIDDLE AGES
PIZARRO AND THE CONQUEST OF PERU
FERDINAND AND ISABELLA
CHARLEMAGNE
CHARLES DARWIN AND THE ORIGIN OF SPECIES
RUSSIA IN REVOLUTION
DESERT WAR IN NORTH AFRICA
THE BATTLE OF WATERLOO
THE HOLY LAND IN THE TIME OF JESUS
THE SPANISH ARMADA
BUILDING THE SUEZ CANAL
MOUNTAIN CONQUEST
PHARAOHS OF EGYPT
LEONARDO DA VINCI
THE FRENCH REVOLUTION
CORTES AND THE AZTEC CONQUEST
CAESAR
THE UNIVERSE OF GALILEO AND NEWTON
THE VIKINGS
MARCO POLO'S ADVENTURES IN CHINA
SHAKESPEARE'S ENGLAND
CAPTAIN COOK AND THE SOUTH PACIFIC
THE SEARCH FOR EARLY MAN
JOAN OF ARC
EXPLORATION OF AFRICA
NELSON AND THE AGE OF FIGHTING SAIL
ALEXANDER THE GREAT
RUSSIA UNDER THE CZARS
HEROES OF POLAR EXPLORATION
KNIGHTS OF THE CRUSADES

American Heritage also publishes
AMERICAN HERITAGE JUNIOR LIBRARY
books, a similar series on American history.
Titles now available are:

LABOR ON THE MARCH, THE STORY OF AMERICA'S UNIONS
THE BATTLE OF THE BULGE
THE BATTLE OF YORKTOWN
THE HISTORY OF THE ATOMIC BOMB
TO THE PACIFIC WITH LEWIS AND CLARK
THEODORE ROOSEVELT, THE STRENUOUS LIFE
GEORGE WASHINGTON AND THE MAKING OF A NATION
CAPTAINS OF INDUSTRY
CARRIER WAR IN THE PACIFIC
JAMESTOWN: FIRST ENGLISH COLONY
AMERICANS IN SPACE
ABRAHAM LINCOLN IN PEACE AND WAR
AIR WAR AGAINST HITLER'S GERMANY
IRONCLADS OF THE CIVIL WAR
THE ERIE CANAL
THE MANY WORLDS OF BENJAMIN FRANKLIN
COMMODORE PERRY IN JAPAN
THE BATTLE OF GETTYSBURG
ANDREW JACKSON, SOLDIER AND STATESMAN
ADVENTURES IN THE WILDERNESS
LEXINGTON, CONCORD AND BUNKER HILL
CLIPPER SHIPS AND CAPTAINS
D-DAY, THE INVASION OF EUROPE
WESTWARD ON THE OREGON TRAIL
THE FRENCH AND INDIAN WARS
GREAT DAYS OF THE CIRCUS
STEAMBOATS ON THE MISSISSIPPI
COWBOYS AND CATTLE COUNTRY
TEXAS AND THE WAR WITH MEXICO
THE PILGRIMS AND PLYMOUTH COLONY
THE CALIFORNIA GOLD RUSH
PRIATES OF THE SPANISH MAIN
TRAPPERS AND MOUNTAIN MEN
MEN OF SCIENCE AND INVENTION
NAVAL BATTLES AND HEROES
THOMAS JEFFERSON AND HIS WORLD
DISCOVERERS OF THE NEW WORLD
RAILROADS IN THE DAYS OF STEAM
INDIANS OF THE PLAINS
THE STORY OF YANKEE WHALING

A HORIZON CARAVEL BOOK

THE SEARCH FOR
KING ARTHUR

By the Editors of
HORIZON MAGAZINE

Author
CHRISTOPHER HIBBERT

Consultant
CHARLES THOMAS

Professor of Archaeology, University of Leicester

Published by American Heritage Publishing Co., Inc.
Book Trade and Institutional Distribution by
Harper & Row

FIRST EDITION
Library of Congress Catalog Card Number: 77-91594
Standard Book Number: (trade edition) 8281-5016-8; (library edition) 8281-8014-8
© 1969 by American Heritage Publishing Co., Inc., 551 Fifth Avenue, New York, New
York. 10017. All rights reserved under Berne and Pan-American Copyright Conventions.
Trademark CARAVEL registered United States Patent Office

FOREWORD

The romances about King Arthur and his Knights of the Round Table are probably the best-known legends in the Western world. For most of us they have served as an introduction to the world of chivalry—of knights errant seeking honor and glory on difficult quests, of beauteous ladies watching their lovers joust in brilliant tournaments. It is a world that seems far removed from our own technologically advanced but uncertain times.

The true fascination of the Arthurian legend lies in the fact that their hero is not a myth but an actual historical figure who lived on the island of Britain some fourteen centuries ago in times that were, like our own, full of threats. With the crumbling of the Roman Empire, the people of Britain found themselves conducting a desperate defense of their island against Saxon invaders from across the North Sea. The pagan Saxons killed, looted, and burned; eventually, they took over larger and larger areas and gradually destroyed what remained of the Romano-British, Christianized civilization.

In his search for the historical personage of Arthur, Christopher Hibbert brings those troubled times vividly to life. As his intriguing story makes clear, the actual facts about Arthur are very few and more than a little obscure. But enough is known to build a convincing picture of the sixth-century British warrior who was to become a legend all over the world. The speed with which this legend spread and the astonishing richness of the material that embellished such meager historical facts are themselves tributes to Arthur's power to rally brave men to his cause.

Mr. Hibbert's relating of the quest for Arthur includes a comprehensive account—richly illustrated by manuscript illuminations, paintings, and engravings—of the many changes that the Arthurian legend has undergone over the centuries as fresh generations of troubadours, painters, and poets reinterpreted and embroidered the old tales to suit their needs.

Recent years have seen renewed interest in Arthur, both because of the musical *Camelot*, which has retold the legend in terms of our modern human experience, and because of the archaeological excavations that currently are taking place at South Cadbury Castle in Somerset, England—a site identified with Arthur's Camelot since the sixteenth century. Mr. Hibbert describes the work undertaken there, which has disclosed that the ancient British hill fort was indeed reoccupied around the beginning of the sixth century—the period in which we believe Arthur to have lived. The most recent reports reveal that excavators there have traced the outlines of a sixth-century feasting hall, which they hope may yet be proved to have been used by Arthur and his warriors.

THE EDITORS

A stern and regal Arthur is portrayed in this detail from a French tapestry made around 1385. The Once and Future King usually was identified in medieval art by three crowns, seen here on the pennant and on the gown.

METROPOLITAN MUSEUM OF ART, NEW YORK

RIGHT: *This fourteenth-century German statue of King Arthur was one of a set of sculptures of the Nine Worthies; it was destroyed by bombs during World War II.*

COVER: *Arthur and the Knights of the Round Table set out in search of the Holy Grail in a manuscript illustration made in Italy in the fourteenth century.*

ENDSHEETS: *In another Italian illustration, King Arthur greets a visiting knight at Camelot as Lancelot and Queen Guinevere hold a tryst behind his back.*

TITLE PAGE: *Arthur fights the giant of Mont-Saint-Michel in an illustration from a twelfth-century Flemish copy of Geoffrey of Monmouth's British history.*

BACK COVER: *A fourteenth-century French manuscript about Merlin contains this miniature of King Arthur and his knights pursuing a fleet-footed stag.*

CONTENTS

An attempt to kill Arthur (left, foreground) is thwarted in this four-teenth-century illustration. At right, Sir Gawain topples the assailant.

LEGENDS AND LEGACIES

In the heart of the quiet, gentle countryside of southwest England is a yellow limestone hill. It rises suddenly and sharply five hundred feet above the little village of South Cadbury, and old men who have lived all their lives in its shadow have strange tales to tell. South Cadbury Castle is a hollow hill, so they say, and if on St. John's Eve you could find the golden gates that lead inside it, there you would discover King Arthur sitting in the middle of his court. Sometimes on rough winter nights you can hear the king trot by with his hounds along the well-worn track, for, as one old man put it, "folks do say that on the night of the full moon King Arthur and his men ride round the hill, and their horses are shod with silver and a silver shoe has been found in the track where they do ride, and when they have ridden round the hill, they stop to water their horses at the Wishing Well."

For countless generations such legends have been told of Arthur, the "Once and Future King," and of his noble knights. Not only at South Cadbury, which has long been identified with Arthur's palace of Camelot, but all over England, Wales, and Scotland as well, his fame survives in strange myths of unknown antiquity.

Each county has its own legends. In Cornwall the tale goes that all the farmlands and the forests "swarmed with giants until Arthur, the good king, vanished them all with his cross-sword." In Northumberland, beneath the castle of Sewingshields, Arthur and his queen, Guinevere, their knights and their ladies, and the king's pack of hounds all lie sleeping in the vaults. So, too, do they sleep beneath the ruins of Richmond Castle in Yorkshire, waiting to be wakened by the blast of a horn that lies on a table by the entrance to their cavern. An unwary farmer once stumbled across them, it is said, but lacked the courage to blow the horn that would bring them back to life. Wales is full of tales of caves and hollow hills in which Arthur and his knights await the call to return. One day, all these legends

One of the most impressive sites named for Arthur is the hill known as Arthur's Seat (left), whose lion-shaped bulk dominates the city of Edinburgh. From its summit, the tradition goes, King Arthur watched his army defeat the Picts. The map at right identifies most of the places mentioned in this chapter; more detailed maps appear on pages 61, 67, and 115.

agree, King Arthur will be roused from his long slumber and ride forth to save his people, at a time when they most need him.

As well as the legends, there are place names. Arthur, it seems, traveled far and wide, for his name can be found the length and breadth of the country—from the Scilly islands of Great and Little Arthur off the southwestern coast of Cornwall, to Arthur's Seat, looming above Scotland's capital city of Edinburgh, far to the north; and from Arthur's Chair high in the hills of Breconshire in Wales to Arthur's Hill at Newcastle, on the northeastern coast of Northumberland. No other name in the whole of Britain turns up so frequently, in fact—except that of the Devil. No one knows exactly how old most of these place names are, just as no one knows how old the legends are. But somewhere in the dark mists of history beyond the time of their creation there was a real Arthur who inspired them.

The Arthur who has become part of the fabric of our lives today is mostly a creation of medieval times, when troubadours and chroniclers made him into a hero of romance, a Christian champion, a noble ruler whose knights were patterns of chivalry. These Arthurian tales have taken their place in our literature, and over the centuries poets and painters have created the characters and their adventures anew. The myth has become so real to us, in fact, that we tend to forget the existence of an actual, historical

N

NORTH SEA

IRISH
SEA

ATLANTIC

OCEAN

ENGLISH   CHANNEL

BRISTOL
CHANNEL

SCILLY
ISLES

NORMANDY

BRITTANY

ARGYLL

Edinburgh
LOTHIAN

NORTH-
UMBERLAND

Richmond

YORKSHIRE

ULSTER

LEINSTER
Dublin

St. Asaph   Chester
            Newcastle

Lincoln

WARWICK
WORCESTER

HEREFORD
BRECON

Monmouth   Oxford

Caerleon

ESSEX

BERKSHIRE   London
Bath   Windsor
WILTSHIRE

SOMERSET

Cadbury   Winchester

KENT
Dover

Tintagel

DEVON   DORSET   Southampton   SUSSEX

Calais

CORNWALL

Mont St. Michel

0   25   50   75
Scale of Miles

13

uint au gue palier li leterirent
en lestour · la ueissies ces cheualier
gesir parmi laigue qui la estoit
toute rouge del sanc des mors ·

Et keus nuit si angoisseuseu
atoute lensengne quil empo
toit· Et quant li·x·rois uj

The medieval artist forgot to draw in Arthur's lance in this illumination, in which the king (left) unhorses
one of ten rebels who claimed the throne. The dragon banner proclaims Arthur's descent from Uther Pendragon.

Arthur. He may not have been a king in the sense we understand kingship. He may not have been even a particularly good or generous or idealistic man. All we know, in starting out to search for him, is that he must have been a remarkable person, because fame does not come without good reason, and Arthur's fame never has been equaled.

The earliest known reference to a historical Arthur is an indirect one, dating from the turbulent centuries immediately after A.D. 410, when the last Roman garrison was withdrawn from Britain, the westernmost outpost of a Roman Empire that was crumbling into decay. Following the legions' departure, the island suffered constant invasions by Jutes, Angles, and Saxons from across the North Sea, and in an epic poem written about 603, the Welsh bard Aneurin describes one of the many battles that took place between these invaders and the Britons, fighting desperately to repel them. From this long poem, *Gododdin*, it appears that Arthur's name already was identified with outstanding courage, for Aneurin describes the feats of a certain British hero by saying that his valor was remarkable, "although he was no Arthur."

Another significant clue is this. A century before *Gododdin* was written, the name Arthur was virtually unknown in Britain. By the late sixth and early seventh centuries, however, it had become fairly common, for there are four or five Arthurs to be traced even in the scanty records that have come down to us from this period. One of them was a prince of Argyll, who was born to the Scottish king Aedán mac Gabráin about 570; another Arthur was born at much the same time in southwestern Wales, great-grandson of a ruler named Vortiporius, to whom a monument still exists; while in 620 the Irish king Morgan was killed by one "Artuir, son of Bicoir, a Briton." It is difficult to account for this sudden popularity of the name unless a real Arthur existed at this time, or shortly before, whose exploits had so excited the admiration of his contemporaries that several British leaders named their sons in his honor.

Yet although these references strongly suggest that a historical Arthur was living in Britain some time during the sixth century, the sources from that period do not mention his name directly. It is not until some two hundred fifty years later, in fact, that Arthur's name first appears in an authentic chronicle: the *Historia Brittonum*, which was compiled in Latin by a Welsh monk named Nennius in the ninth century. In a series of tantalizingly brief references Nennius mentions Arthur as the British victor in a series of sixth-century battles fought by the Britons against the Saxons. Nennius gives very little solid information, as we shall see in a later chapter, but he does confirm Arthur's legendary reputation for bravery, suggested by the allusion in the poem *Gododdin*; more important, he makes clear that Arthur was a figure around whom fantastic legends already had begun to cluster.

Nennius recounts two stories that illustrate this; justly, he calls them *mirabilia*—marvels. The first concerns Carn Cabal, a cairn, or monument, made from stones piled on top of each other, in the Welsh county of Breconshire. On the top of the cairn was a stone bearing the footprint of Arthur's dog, Cabal, who had so marked it by treading on it during a boar hunt. Arthur had caused the cairn to be built as a memorial to his beloved dog; and whenever the stone with the footprint was removed, unfailingly within twenty-four hours it would be back again on its heap.

The other story was of the miraculous tomb of Arthur's son Anir, who was buried beside the source of the River Gamber in Herefordshire on the Welsh border. Anir "was the son of Arthur the soldier," Nennius writes, "and Arthur himself killed him there and buried him. And when men come to measure the length of the mound, they find it sometimes six feet, sometimes nine, sometimes twelve, and sometimes fifteen. Whatever length you find it at one time, you will find it different at another, and I myself have proved this to be true."

Fanciful as Nennius' stories may appear, they were far outdone in the early twelfth century, when a scholar known as Geoffrey of Monmouth wrote a book called *Historia Regum Britanniae* (*A History of the Kings of Britain*). In it he gave himself the task of providing an account of "the kings who dwelt in Britain before the coming of Christ," and "especially of King Arthur and the many others who succeeded him after the coming of Christ." Geoffrey probably was born in Monmouth, in South Wales, although he may originally have been of Breton stock; all we know of his parentage for certain is that his father, interestingly enough, was called Arthur. He ended his life as bishop of St. Asaph, a town in North Wales. Twelfth-century Wales and Brittany both were areas where most of the inhabitants were of Celtic origin, which means that they were descended from the original Britons who peopled the island in Roman times. Geoffrey was an imaginative man who was proud of his origins; he also was a well-read and ambitious man who shared the heritage of the Normans who were Brit-

In a scene cleverly enclosed in an initial letter from a thirteenth-century French manuscript, Arthur sits at a table while some of his knights plan their next quest.

Above is a section of a page from an early copy of Geoffrey of Monmouth's fanciful History of the Kings of Britain, *which was written during the twelfth century.*

ain's overlords at the time. His *History of the Kings of Britain* combines these influences; thanks to Geoffrey's ability as a writer, it presents the Arthurian legend in a way that appealed to a far wider audience than the Norman noblemen to whom it was dedicated.

The *History* is divided into twelve books, three of which are devoted to King Arthur, and it is quite clear from reading the work that it is he who excites the author's imagination above all the other British kings. Here, for the first time in a written work, Arthur appears as the great romantic hero of Celtic tradition, with a splendid court, a magical sword, a shield painted with the likeness of the Blessed Mary, Mother of God, a spear "thirsty for slaughter," and a helmet whose crest is "carved in the shape of a dragon." His court is as magnificent and as well conducted as that of the Emperor Charlemagne, and its atmosphere is pervaded with twelfth-century chivalric ideals. "For none was thought worthy of a lady's love, unless he had been three times approved in the bearing of arms. And so the ladies were made chaste and the knights the better by their loves."

Here, in Geoffrey's *History of the Kings of Britain* the main traditions of the Arthurian epic are established for the first time, and the stories first told that subsequently would become so well known. Here, too, is the first appearance of the legend that Arthur did not merely defeat the Saxons, but led British armies overseas on triumphant campaigns that

ranged from Ireland to the borders of Italy, bringing them victories worthy of those won by Caesar himself.

According to Geoffrey of Monmouth, his wonderful—or as many were to say, incredible—narrative was based upon "a very ancient book in the British tongue." This had been brought to England from Wales by his friend Walter, Archdeacon of Oxford, "a man well informed about the history of foreign countries, and most learned in all branches of history." Because no one at the time—other than Geoffrey and Walter—appears ever to have seen this ancient book and no Welsh or Breton chronicle that in the least resembles it ever has been discovered, it has long been supposed that Geoffrey simply invented it. Certainly, it was customary in those days, when compiling a history whose accuracy might be questioned, to claim that its authority was vouched for by a learned work of great antiquity. In any case, Geoffrey of Monmouth ended his book with the note that he has left the work of retelling the biographies of the later Welsh and Saxon kings to three other historians who were his contemporaries. Perhaps he expected them also to be his critics, because he recommends that they "say nothing at all about the kings of the Britons, since they have not in their possession the book in the British language which Walter, Archdeacon of Oxford, brought from Wales. It is this book which I have been at such pains to translate thus into Latin, for it was composed very accurately about the deeds of these princes and to their honor."

One historian undeterred by this warning was William of Newburgh, who was born about 1136, the year Geoffrey finished his *History*, and himself subsequently wrote a history of English affairs from the Norman Conquest onward. A far more critical historian than Geoffrey, William strongly condemned his predecessor's work as fanciful, remarking that if the events it related ever happened, they must have taken place in a different world. Geoffrey, according to William, had made "the little finger of his Arthur thicker than the loins of Alexander the Great." Similarly, another chronicler, writing in the fourteenth century, wondered how it could have come about that Arthur's conquest of thirty kingdoms and his assault upon a Roman emperor should have been overlooked by all Continental historians.

Following Geoffrey of Monmouth's account of Arthur's conquest of thirty kingdoms, a fourteenth-century English chronicle portrays the king astride the crowns of exactly thirty countries, some of them mythical, some real.

Later historians generally have agreed with these early skeptics in disbelieving the tale about the ancient book found in Wales by the Archdeacon of Oxford. They supposed that Geoffrey based his stories not so much on Nennius' *Historia Brittonum* or on any such recognized authority on early British history, nor even so much on confused national and local traditions, as on his own colorful imagination. It has been noted that Geoffrey's *History* appeared in the troubled reign of King Stephen when the Norman dynasty that ruled England was in danger of losing its power and influence. Its members felt the need for a distinguished and glorious predecessor on the throne. Charlemagne, the precursor and inspiration of the kings of France and Germany, already was an accepted folk hero who,

Medieval readers revered three pagan, three Hebrew, and three Christian heroes as the Nine Worthies of the World. One of the Christians was Arthur, usually identified—as in this line-up, where he stands third from right with Charlemagne on his left—by a banner that bears three crowns.

legend said, was not dead but only sleeping, waiting to return in triumph with his paladins. A relationship with the legendary Arthur could greatly benefit the Norman kings in their efforts to throw off French domination.

Other historians have stressed the fact that Geoffrey of Monmouth was brought up in Wales and in the atmosphere of Celtic lore and that while flattering the royal court by presenting Arthur as the ideal of an Anglo-Norman king, he also was flattering the Celts by exaggerating the splendors of their own past. In fact, he was not really writing history at all, but a tract that would demonstrate the heroic virtues of the British race and their leaders by recounting their stupendous victories over all their enemies.

Yet Geoffrey of Monmouth occupies a very important place in this story. For it was he who first created an Arthurian legend that fired the imagination of the whole of Christendom. In his own country his success was immediate. The enormous popularity of his work can be judged from the fact that nearly two hundred full manuscripts of it have survived, some fifty of which actually date from the twelfth century. Throughout the Middle Ages Geoffrey's *History* remained the primary source for all writers about Celtic Britain.

But it was on the Continent that the legend was most widely expanded and embellished. As early as the 1140's, Geoffrey Gaimar had translated Geoffrey's *History* from Latin into French; and in 1155 the Anglo-Norman poet Maistre Wace brought out a verse paraphrase, *Le Roman de Brut* (named for a totally mythical Brutus of Troy who, in Geoffrey's account, was the founder of Britain). This makes the story even more dramatic and romantic, introducing the legend of the Round Table, around which Arthur's knights sit in feast and conference, and presenting Arthur as "a lover of glory, whose famous deeds are right fit to be kept in remembrance: he ordained the courtesies of courts, and observed high state in a very splendid fashion."

Around 1175 the Arthurian legend was taken up by the French poet Chrétien de Troyes. A skillful compiler of romances for the French feudal aristocracy, Chrétien added to the stories fresh characters and a fresh flavor, casting the tales in a strangely unreal, ethereal setting in which love was a kind of religion. In this he was responding to the wishes of his patroness, Countess Marie de Champagne, whose brilliant court was the center for this new code of courtly love. It glorified an ideal kind of affection between a knight and his lady—who could not be his wife, since all

Another favorite medieval concept was that of the blind goddess Fortune and her wheel, whose uncertain movements could whirl a man from fame to insecurity in a moment. In this illumination, made in 1316, when the Arthurian legend was most popular, Fortune holds a wheel with Arthur enthroned and past favorites clinging to its sides.

The earliest depictions of Arthur known to us today are both Italian. The archivolt above, from Modena, dates from the early twelfth century; in it Winlogee (Breton for Guinevere) has been imprisoned in a castle by the villains Burmaltus, Mardoc, and Carrado, while Artus de Bretani and five of his knights ride to her rescue. An 1165 mosaic from Otranto (right) shows "Rex Arturus" mounted on a goat, which may allude to Arthur's legendary overlordship of the Antipodes, supposedly an underground realm of dwarfs whose tiny rulers used goats instead of horses.

marriages were "arranged" in those days and true love within a relationship of duty was out of the question. The ideals of courtly love were that the lover should be humble and courteous and revere and obey his lady almost as if she were his lord. In return, the lady would reward his devotion by loving him as completely as she cared to. Understandably, the ideals of courtly love became extremely popular and the stories that glorified it were read and recited all over Europe.

Following Chrétien's example, several other French writers produced prose and verse romances, some largely imitative, others containing an altered version of an old story or a freshly interpolated tale, and began grouping them together. Storytellers from Brittany almost certainly added to the increasing body of material with their detailed accounts of Arthurian adventures, based on the old Celtic tales of marvels and magic, which they retold as they wandered from one nobleman's hall to the next.

Meanwhile, in England, a Worcestershire priest named Layamon translated Wace's *Roman de Brut* from French into English, once again expanding and elaborating the basic material. In Layamon's *Brut*, the first version of the Arthurian legend to be written in English, the emphasis changes once more: Layamon was writing not for the aristocracy, whose language was still French, but for the common people of England, who spoke an antique form of the language that we ourselves use and were interested chiefly in the characters and adventures already familiar to them from their native heritage. Layamon treats the legend as an epic of early Britain in which Arthur is a practical, nationalistic, somewhat barbaric leader, very different from

the kind of magical fairy king who appears in the French romances. This earthier, more straightforward Arthur is an essentially British hero, and this treatment of him is carried on in several later poems and prose romances written in English that retell the adventures of the king and his knights.

Strangely enough, the first appearance of King Arthur in a work of art now extant was not in his native realm of Britain, but in Italy, far to the south, where a relief of Arthur and his knights was carved above the north doorway of Modena Cathedral some time between 1099 and 1120. In 1165 Arturus Rex again was depicted, this time on a mosaic pavement in the cathedral of Otranto, on the southern heel of Italy. The mosaic portrays the king bearing a scepter and riding a goat, which seems a rather odd mount for a king—except that goats at that time had some association with those who ruled subterranean kingdoms, as Arthur was supposed to do.

About thirty years after this pavement was laid down, an English visitor to the island of Sicily, not far distant, reported that its inhabitants believed that King Arthur could be found in the volcanic depths below Mount Etna. He also had been seen on a Sicilian plain by a groom in search of a runaway horse. This man had crossed the plain, entered

TEXT CONTINUED ON PAGE 26

23

LANCELOT: CHAMPION OF COURTLY LOVE

As each generation of storytellers and artists has retold the Arthurian legend, emphases have shifted and fresh heroes have been given prominence. But Lancelot has been the most famous of Arthur's knights since the twelfth century, when Countess Marie de Champagne commissioned a romance glorifying courtly love, with Lancelot as its hero. In later versions Lancelot was abducted as an infant by the Lady of the Lake and raised by her as a paragon of courtly behavior. (Above, in a fifteenth-century drawing, Lancelot plays chess with Tristram, left, in the Lady's palace.) Once he had arrived at King Arthur's court, Lancelot fell in love with Guinevere and strove so hard to be worthy of her that she finally granted him a chaperoned assignation —and a kiss (above, opposite). Later, when Guinevere was kidnapped by another admirer, Lancelot crossed a bridge made from a sword, fought two lions, and defeated her abductor, as depicted at right in a fourteenth-century French illustration. Incredibly, his reward on that occasion was not thanks but scorn, because he had hesitated briefly in one small test of devotion. The lovers soon reconciled, however, and resumed the relationship that eventually was to bring about the ruin of the Round Table.

a marvelous palace, and there had found King Arthur lying on a bed. The king told him of his last battle and that each year, on the anniversary of that battle, his wounds broke out afresh. It seems surprising that the tradition of Arthur's survival should have traveled so far from its British origins, but the island of Sicily was ruled at this time by a Norman dynasty and the legend could well have been imported by storytellers in their service and instantly transplanted into a Mediterranean setting by their eager listeners.

Within two centuries the legend of King Arthur and his knights had spread all over Europe and even into parts of Asia. In France Arthur's fame almost eclipsed that of Charlemagne, who was not restored to his former pre-eminent position until after the Middle Ages had drawn to a close. In Germany the finest medieval poets celebrated Arthur's great deeds and the adventures of his knights, particularly Tristram and Percival. In Italy Dante wrote of Lancelot. From Ireland to Greece there were translations of Arthurian texts. His was a familiar name throughout the Low Countries, in Scandinavia and Switzerland, Spain and Portugal, Cyprus and Sicily.

"Whither has not flying fame spread the name of Arthur the Briton?" asked an English writer as early as the 1170's. "Even as far as the empire of Christendom extends. Who, I say, does not speak of Arthur the Briton, since he is almost better known to the people of Asia than to the *Britanni*, as our pilgrims returning from the East inform us. The Eastern people speak of him, as do the Western, though separated by the width of the whole earth."

Early in the thirteenth century noblemen and knights began amusing themselves with festivities that came to be called Round Tables, in honor of the great table around which Arthur's knights had sat at Camelot. The idea of a round table that would make no distinction between the ranks of the knights who sat at it seemed to have a particular appeal to the medieval mind—no doubt in contrast to the strict rules of precedence that governed every other activity, especially eating in company. Crusaders who battled in earnest to free the Holy Land from Moslem domination also disported themselves with jousts and banquets

This herald carrying the banners of four judges named to preside at a joust is from a fifteenth-century book of tournament ceremonial. It was written by René I of Naples and Anjou, who has been called the last of the troubadours.

The poems and romances that recounted the pleasures and pains of courtly love spread rapidly from one country to another. This illustration, from a collection of troubadour love lyrics made in Germany, shows a lady rewarding the devotion of a knight—who continues feeding his falcon.

The medieval passion for jousting led to many chivalric encounters inspired by the Arthurian legend. At St. Inglevert, near Calais, in 1390 three French noblemen held the lists for thirty days against all comers, and foreign knights flocked to challenge them. Above, a knight wearing his lady's veil (left) encounters another at lance-point; behind them are squires with fresh lances, and at rear more knights await their turn to tilt before a crowd of spectators.

A few days later, in the huge courtyard of the castle's Upper Ward, work began on the building of a great stone hall for the Round Table, where the knights of the fellowship could in future hold their feasts. Soon afterward it had to be suspended, for the King went to war with France once more and could not afford the double expense. He returned to Windsor in 1347, triumphant after his crushing victory over the French at Crécy and his capture of the port of Calais, the key to the English Channel. The unfinished hall for the knights of the Round Table still stood in the Upper Ward to remind him of his intentions. Edward was a man of great ambition, who took his obligations as a knight and as a leader of knights more seriously than his responsibility as sovereign. Pleasure and feasting occupied him only for a while. Soon he was considering an enterprise "more particular and more select," the revival of his idea for a fellowship of knights that would be the envy of Europe.

So it was that the Round Table of King Arthur became the original inspiration of the Order of the Garter. This order, which took its name from the badges worn by the knights who competed in a tournament held at Windsor in 1348, was to become, and still remains, in the twentieth century, the most noble and respected order of knighthood in Europe.

By the time the order was founded, however, the ideas of chivalry already were dying. Battles were no longer to be won by sheer bravery, by knights fighting each other with sword and lance. Edward III's own victory at Crécy had proved that a quantity of low-born English longbowmen, posted advantageously, could gain a victory over a knightly army twice the size, despite its superior armor and aristocratic birth. At Agincourt, in 1415, the lesson was hammered home still more strongly when a French army fifty thousand strong clashed with an English force of thirteen thousand. Thousands of French knights, the glory of the chivalry of King Charles VI, disdained to allow a place in the front line to inferior troops and the new and despised artillery. Dismounted, in a dense metal wedge, unable to move in the muddy fields, they were at the mercy of the English archers and men-at-arms. The Englishmen, with freedom to maneuver, simply tumbled the French knights to the ground in their heavy, suffocating armor and chopped them to pieces with their own swords and battle-axes.

Within another half-century England itself was to be torn asunder by civil war as the brutal Wars of the Roses convulsed the country. The Middle Ages were drawing to a close; new ideas, new ways of life, new inventions were being introduced. In 1476 William Caxton set up the first printing press in England and began to print for a growing audience books that previously had been available only in laboriously copied manuscript: Chaucer's *Canterbury Tales*, translations from the classics, an encyclopaedia of philosophy.

On July 31, 1485, Caxton published his sixty-second title from the sign of the Red Pale in the London parish of Westminster. Within a month the first Tudor king of England would ascend the throne; a new era, a Tudor era, was about to begin. Yet the book Caxton printed that July was the most renowned of all medieval romances, Sir Thomas Malory's *Le Morte d'Arthur*—a book that looked back with a kind of nostalgic longing to the glories and heroic achievements of a more chivalrous age, to a strange, past world, already forgotten and idealized.

AND JOYOUS BOOK"

Caxton called it a "noble and joyous book," and so it is. But *Le Morte d'Arthur* is far more than that. It is full of a strange sense of doom that foreshadows the "dolorous death and departing out of this world" of its great hero and his valiant knights. Its author was a prisoner when he wrote it, a prisoner who longed for the day of his deliverance—and that is almost all that we know of him. He probably was Sir Thomas Malory, a Warwickshire gentleman who at one time served as Member of Parliament for his county. Later, however, he apparently turned to a life of crime. A long series of accusations of rape, robbery, cattle thieving, extortion of money by threats, and attempted murder are recorded against him, and he certainly was imprisoned for some years in Newgate jail in London. It seems strange that such a lawless character should be the author of a book full of knightly adventures and noble deeds. But in the troubled times of the Wars of the Roses many men spent long years in prison, and the fact that Malory was accused of these crimes does not necessarily mean that he was guilty of them. There is no record of a trial or of sentence being passed upon him.

Some historians, however, prefer to believe that *Le Morte d'Arthur* was written by a Thomas Malory of Studley and Hutton in Yorkshire while he was a prisoner-of-war in France. It also is possible that its author was neither of these men but yet another Thomas Malory, whose identity remains to be discovered. All that can be said with certainty is that in *Le Morte d'Arthur* he wrote a masterpiece, the one and only medieval romance that has retained its hold on the imagination of five centuries of readers, right down to the present day. Skillfully, painstakingly, the prisoner-

Galahad, who will occupy the Round Table's vacant seat, is introduced to Arthur and his knights. The famous table is conveniently ring-shaped in this picture, so that the tiny blue-clad pages can serve up the feast.

33

knight labored to gather its threads together from the count-less existing Arthurian romances—some French, some English, some in verse, some in prose; and this is the story that he told:

In the days when Uther Pendragon was king of all England, there lived in Cornwall a mighty duke, the Duke of Tintagel, who had a most beautiful wife named Igrayne. The king fell in love with Igrayne, and one day when she was a guest in the royal palace, he took her aside and asked her to sleep with him. But Igrayne was good as well as beautiful and she refused him. Then she told her husband what the king had proposed and begged him to take her from the palace that very night and to ride with her through the darkness to their own castle.

They secretly departed; and when they had gone, the king, in his great anger and burning desire for Igrayne, fell sick. His knights believed that only one man could cure him of his distress, and that was the wizard Merlin. Merlin was sent for, and when he came to the king, he announced that he could, indeed, make him better and that he even could arrange for him to make love to Igrayne; but there was one condition: "The first night that you shall lie by Igrayne you shall get a child on her; and when that child is born, then you must deliver it to me for me to nourish and look after."

The king agreed; and then Merlin said to him, "Now make you ready. This night you shall lie with Igrayne in

OXFORD UNIVERSITY PRESS

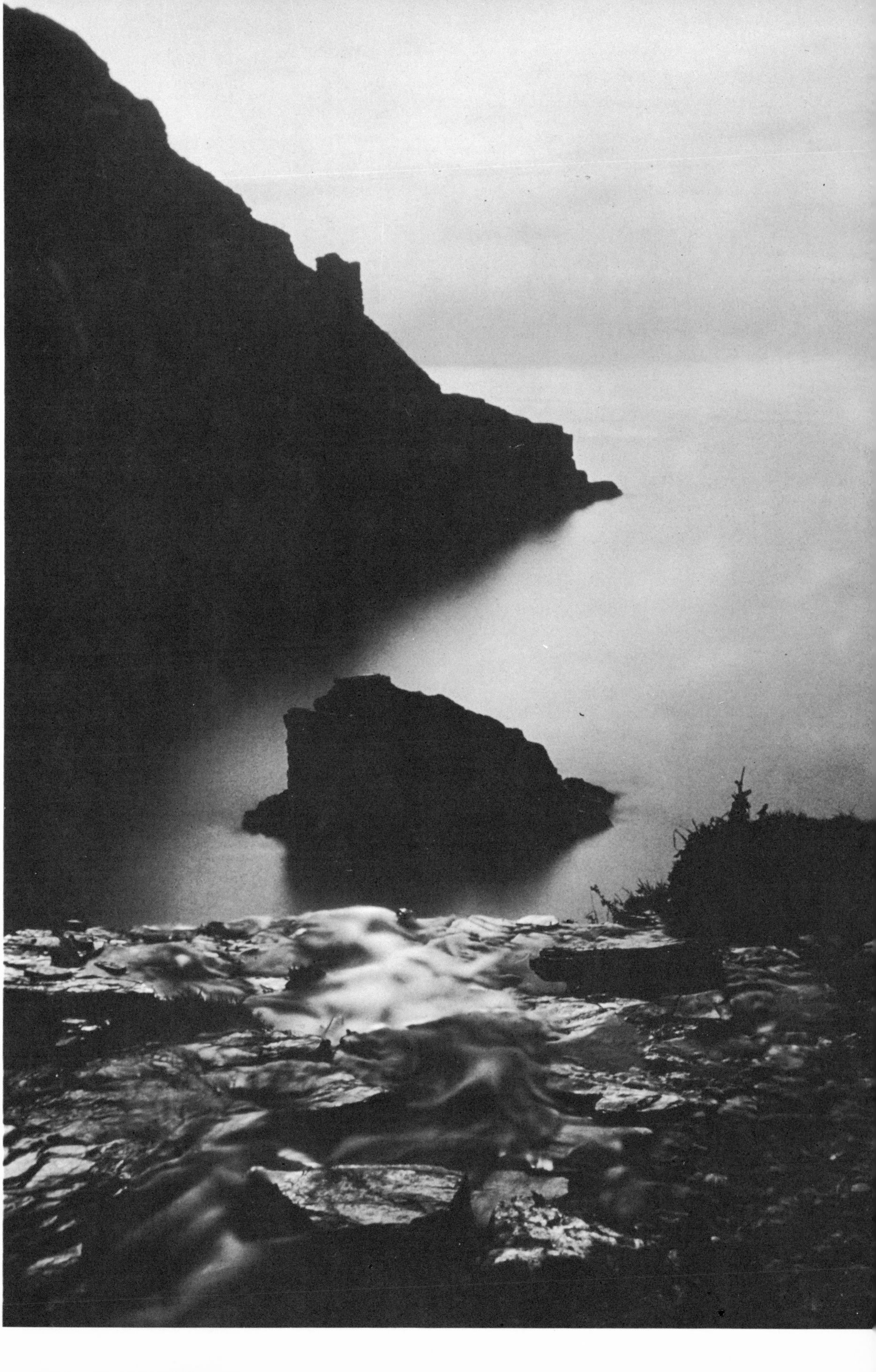

Weekend Telegraph, LONDON: PHOTO, DON STARTUP

The 1468 marriage of Margaret of York to the Duke of Burgundy had artistic as well as political results in England. One of them was William Caxton's introduction of the new craft of printing; another was an increasing use of Flemish artists. This illumination, from an English chronicle decorated in Flanders, shows Arthur's father, Uther, receiving advice from Merlin (left) while the Saxons stand menacingly at right. The significance of the prominent white dog is unknown.

the castle of Tintagel, and you shall be made by magic to look like the duke, her husband." Thus, in the guise of the duke, the king rode to Tintagel and was welcomed by Igrayne to her bed. In due time the baby was born, as Merlin had foretold, and in accordance with the promise King Uther had made, the child was wrapped in cloth of gold and handed over to the care of the wizard. Merlin, in turn, entrusted him to Sir Ector, a true and honest knight and the lord of fine estates in England and Wales. Sir Ector's wife fed him at her breast; and they called a priest to christen him, and the name they gave him was Arthur.

The years passed, King Uther died, and England stood in danger of civil war because the great barons could not agree on who should succeed him. On Merlin's advice, the Archbishop of Canterbury sent for all the quarreling lords and gentlemen-at-arms to come to London at Christmas time and pray to Jesus to show them by some miracle who had the best right to be king. The lords and gentlemen came to London and went to the greatest church there before daybreak to pray and hear Mass. After they had knelt down, there suddenly appeared in the churchyard a big square marble stone. In the stone was fixed a blacksmith's anvil; in the anvil was a great sword, with its point imbedded in the steel; and around the sword was written in letters of gold:

WHOSO PULLETH OUT THIS SWORD OF THIS STONE AND
ANVIL IS RIGHTWISE KING BORN OF ALL ENGLAND

Then all the people marveled; but not one of the lords who struggled with all their power to pull the sword from the anvil could move it so much as the fraction of an inch.

"The man who can pluck out the sword is not here," the Archbishop pronounced. "But do not doubt that God will make him known."

Now it had been arranged that on New Year's Day the lords and knights should ride into the fields outside the city to compete in a tournament; and it happened that two of the knights attending the tournament were the good Sir Ector and his son Kay, who had been knighted recently and was eager to prove his valor. With them was Kay's young foster brother, Arthur, acting as his squire. As they were riding to the tourney ground, Sir Kay suddenly realized that he foolishly had left his sword behind in his father's London lodgings, and he sent Arthur galloping back to fetch it for him. But when Arthur reached town, he found that the door of the lodgings was locked, for all the servants had left to see the tournament. Then Arthur said to himself, "I will ride to the churchyard and take the sword with me that sticks in the stone; for my brother, Sir Kay, shall not be without a sword this day."

As Malory tells it:

So whan he cam to the chircheyard, sir Arthur alight and tayed his hors to the style, and so he wente to the tente and found no knyghtes there, for they were atte justyng. And so he handled the swerd by the handels, and lightly and fiersly pulled it out of the stone, and took his hors and rode his way untyll he came to his broder sir Kay and delyverd hym the swerd.

As soon as he saw the sword, Sir Ector understood the marvelous thing that Arthur had done, and immediately he rode with him back to London, where he told him to place the sword back in the anvil and pull it out again. Arthur did so; and although all the lords thereafter tried to do as he did, none could move the sword but Arthur. Whereupon all the people cried out with one voice, "We will have Arthur for our king. We will have no more delay. It is God's

Uther Pendragon embraces a somewhat unwilling Igrayne outside the castle of Tintagel. This woodcut is from the first illustrated edition of Le Morte d'Arthur, *published in 1498 by Wynkyn de Worde, who inherited Caxton's printing business after his death.*

will that he shall be our king, and we will kill any man who holds against it."

Then they all knelt down before him, rich and poor alike. Malory goes on:

And Arthur foryaf [forgave] hem and took the swerd bitwene both his handes and offred it upon the aulter where the Archebisshop was, and so was he made knyghte of [by] the best man that was there. And so anon was the coronacyon made, and ther was he sworne unto his lordes and the comyns [common people] for to be a true kyng, to stand with true justyce fro thens forth the dayes of this lyf.*

Now that he was king of England, Arthur set out at the head of his knights to fight against all the evil barons who were oppressing his people and against all the rebel lords who would not accept his right to the crown. Among these rebel lords was King Lot of Lothian and Orkney, who scornfully refused to recognize as king a beardless boy who was not even of royal blood. While Arthur was at war in Wales, King Lot's wife, Morgause, came to his headquarters in the city of Caerleon, pretending to bring him a message, but really to spy upon him.

Now, this Queen Morgause was the daughter of Igrayne and the Duke of Tintagel, and thus she was Arthur's half-sister. But Arthur did not know this, and when Morgause came to him with her four young sons, Gawain, Gaheris, Agravaine, and Gareth, she was so beautiful, so richly dressed, and so desirable, that Arthur "cast great love unto her and desired to lie by her." And so they were agreed, and he begat upon his sister a child, and the name of the child was Mordred.

One day, soon after this, King Arthur was riding with Merlin beside a lake. He had broken his sword in all the fighting he had done, but Merlin told him not to worry— "hereby is a sword that shall be yours if I can." Then Arthur noticed, in the middle of the lake, an arm appearing out of the water and in its hand was a shining sword. Catching sight of a young woman walking by the lake, he said to her, "Damsel, what sword is that yonder that the arm holds above the water? I would it were mine, for I have no sword."

"Sir Arthur," replied the damsel, "that sword is mine

TEXT CONTINUED ON PAGE 42

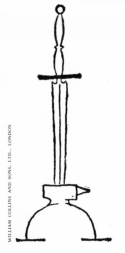

The first edition of The Sword in the Stone, *the initial book in T. H. White's retelling of the Arthurian legend, contained the author's own line drawings. This one illustrates exactly how the sword was stuck into the anvil, which in turn was mounted on the stone.*

*These extracts are taken from the most recent and most authentic edition of Malory's works, edited by Professor Eugène Vinaver and published by the Oxford University Press, on which this whole chapter is based. For easier reading, however, we have retold subsequent quotations in modern English.

The climactic moment when Arthur proves his right to the throne by pulling the sword out of the stone is happily combined in this French illumination, made about 1290, with his offering the sword on the altar at his coronation.

MERLIN: WIZARD AND PROPHET

Merlin enters the Arthurian legend in Geoffrey of Monmouth's *History*, in which he is depicted as a youth whose prophecies cover the centuries up to Geoffrey's own era with remarkable accuracy. He also performs the noteworthy feat of moving the stone circle at Stonehenge from Ireland to its present location on Salisbury Plain (above). A more familiar Merlin is the gray-bearded magician at left in an engraving from a Victorian edition of Spenser's *The Faerie Queene*. The Merlyn who guides Arthur on the path to kingship in T. H. White's *The Once and Future King* is seen at right in a sketch by the author; his pet owl sits atop his head. Both White and Spenser owed much to Malory's *Le Morte d'Arthur*, in which Merlin teaches all his arts to Nimue, his mistress. The result is depicted in the 1498 woodcut at right: she enchants the wizard and locks him up in a cave.

and you shall have it. Go into yonder barge and row yourself to the sword and take it and the scabbard with you." All of which Arthur did accordingly; and he called the sword Excalibur, which means "cut steel."

Armed with Excalibur, King Arthur sailed across the Channel to fight the Roman Emperor Lucius, who had demanded a tribute that the English were not prepared to pay. On his way he stopped to save the people of Normandy from the giant of Mont-St.-Michel, whom he found gnawing on the roasted limbs of newborn babies. "There was never devil in hell more horriblier made" than this giant,

Highlights of Arthur's European campaign were illustrated in England in the 1300's (right) and in Flanders a century later (below). The primitive style of the depictions of Arthur's encounter with the giant of Mont-St.-Michel and his defeat of the Emperor Lucius (near and far right) contrasts with the detailed elegance of Guillaume Vrelant's miniature of Arthur and his large army preparing to attack the city of Rome.

who was thirty feet tall and the foulest sight that ever man saw. He snatched up an iron club and swiped at Arthur so hard that his crown fell off. But Arthur fearlessly grappled with him, "and so they weltered and tumbled over the crags and bushes" until they finally rolled right down the mount to the seashore. And there Arthur plunged a dagger into the giant's ribs and killed him.

Then Arthur marched south into the province of Champagne, and in a great battle there he overwhelmed the Emperor Lucius and killed him with his own hands. With his army, he traveled onward over the mountains into Italy, overcoming all his enemies, Saracens, and monsters as he marched, and was himself crowned emperor in Rome by the Pope. On his return to England he was met by all his court, who escorted him in triumph to Camelot.

King Arthur's knights had long been pressing him to take a wife. When the king sought Merlin's advice, the magician asked him if there was any woman he loved more than another.

"Yea," said King Arthur, "I love Guinevere, daughter of King Leodegrance of Cameliard who holds in his house the Round Table that was given to him by my father, King Uther; and Guinevere is the fairest damsel that I know or could ever find." But Merlin, who had the gift of seeing into the future, warned Arthur against Guinevere. He insisted that she would not be faithful to her husband but would fall in love with his noblest knight, and that this noblest knight, Sir Lancelot, would fall in love with her.

OVERLEAF: *In another miniature by Vrelant, Arthur and Guinevere are married by the Archbishop of Canterbury under a roof fretted with stars. The various knights and ladies are clad in garments fashionable in the 1460's.*

43

Taking a drink at right is the notorious Questing Beast. Searching for the creature was the sole occupation of King Pellinore and Sir Palomides, two knights of the Round Table. The beast, so Malory tells us, had the remarkable ability to make a noise in its belly "like unto the questing of thirty couple hounds," but fortunately for the onlookers who have stumbled upon it here, "all the while the beast drank there was no noise."

Yet Arthur paid no attention; he was determined to take Guinevere for his wife, whatever Merlin said. Therefore, Merlin went to King Leodegrance of Cameliard to tell him of Arthur's desire.

"That is the best tidings that ever I heard," said King Leodegrance, who esteemed Arthur as a most noble and worthy king. "I shall send him a gift that shall please him, for I shall give him the Round Table which Uther, his father, gave me. There are places at it for a hundred and fifty knights, and I shall fill a hundred of those places myself by sending him a hundred good knights."

"Now, Merlin," said King Arthur when he heard this news, "go and find me fifty knights of the most courage and renown in all this land." And Merlin went forth, but he brought only twenty-eight knights back to Camelot because he could find no more who were worthy to sit at the Round Table. One of them was Arthur's nephew Gawain, who was to be knighted on the day of the wedding. And Guinevere and King Arthur were married in the church of St. Stephen at Camelot with great solemnity.

Then the Archbishop of Canterbury was fetched to bless the seats of the Round Table while all the knights were in their places; and after they had risen and gone to pay homage to King Arthur, there was found in every seat, in letters of gold, the name of the knight to whom the place belonged, or would belong, save for two seats, which had no names at all. And Merlin told the king that no knight should sit in those places but those who were the worthiest of all. Each knight was given riches and land and was charged by King Arthur never to commit murder or robbery or do any evil thing, always to grant mercy to those who asked for mercy, and upon pain of death, to go to the help of ladies in distress.

All the knights promised to obey these laws, and all of them were brave and noble men; yet one of them stood out above all the others in nobility and courage, and this was Sir Lancelot of the Lake, son of the king of Benwick. As Merlin had foretold, he performed many chivalrous deeds for Queen Guinevere, "whom he loved above all other ladies all the days of his life." And the queen fell in love with him.

Not only did the knights of the Round Table have to undertake whatever quest befell them, they also had to tell of their adventures afterward. In this miniature, Arthur is questioning a group of knights assembled to recount their quests.

But King Arthur did not know of their love; and he and Sir Lancelot and Sir Lancelot's son, Sir Galahad, and Sir Tristram, Sir Gawain, Sir Gareth, Sir Percival, Sir Bors, and Sir Bedivere and all the other members of the noble fellowship went out upon many adventures and quests. They sought to slay the monstrous Questing Beast; they laid siege to castles; they took part in dangerous battles and exciting tournaments; they strove to gain the love of fair ladies; above all, they endeavored to find the Holy Grail, the holy vessel that Christ Himself used at the Last Supper. It suddenly and mysteriously had appeared one evening at Camelot, covered with rich white silk, and after filling the hall where the king and his knights sat with brilliant light and sweet perfumes, it was borne away suddenly no one knew where. Nearly all the knights joined in the quest for the Holy Grail, to the sorrow both of King Arthur, who feared that they would never afterward return to the Round Table, and of Queen Guinevere, who grieved to see them— and in particular, Sir Lancelot—depart from Camelot. Yet although Sir Lancelot tried with all his strength of body and mind, although he did penances, humbled himself, and wore a hair shirt for more than a year, he never could do more than glimpse the Holy Grail from far off, for no knight could complete the quest who was not completely free from

The quest for the Grail naturally attracted the Round Table's noblest knight, Lancelot, seen at right in blue bidding farewell to King Arthur while Guinevere watches from a balcony. Lancelot's love affair with the queen, which prevented him from succeeding in the quest, was renewed soon after his return, when the lovers arranged a meeting while Arthur was away hunting deer in the forest (left).

sin. Only Sir Galahad, Sir Percival, and Sir Bors were pure enough to be worthy; and after they had successfully found the Grail and mystically achieved the quest, the sacred vessel was borne up to heaven and never seen again.

However hard Sir Lancelot had tried to live honorably and forget his passion for the queen, he found that he could not banish her from his thoughts. Soon after his return from the Grail quest they were meeting secretly once more. "So they loved together more hotter than they did before and had many such secret trysts together that many in the court of Camelot spoke of it." Loudest in their talk against the queen and Lancelot were Sir Gawain's brother Sir Agravaine and his half-brother, Sir Mordred, the king's son. One day in the king's chamber Sir Agravaine said openly, "I marvel that we all be not ashamed both to see and to know how Sir Lancelot lies daily and nightly by the queen. Fall whatsoever fall may, I will disclose it to the king."

True to his threat, Sir Agravaine, accompanied by Sir Mordred, went to the king and told him what people were whispering about the queen and Sir Lancelot, and he urged him to set a trap to catch them out. "My lord," said Sir Agravaine, "you shall ride to-morrow a-hunting, and doubt you not, Lancelot will not go with you. And so when it draws toward night, send word to the queen that you will stay out all night, and send for your cooks. And then upon

a tois eleu; uos cuuoicia deus auiceme
part aufi com il afet espee. Lots regarcet
uers la tue qtreual et uoit ueuu aufi
come abesoing une camoiselle monte
seur un palefroi blac et ueuoit uers
auz gnz aleure.

Surprised by Mordred and his accomplices, Lancelot snatches up his sword while Guinevere wrings her hands. This Victorian impression of the scene in the queen's chamber is by Dante Gabriel Rossetti, who was illustrating The Defence of Guenevere, *a poem by the artist-poet William Morris that pleaded the queen's cause.*

pain of death that night we shall take him with the queen, and we shall bring him to you, alive or dead."

King Arthur was loath to believe them, for he dearly loved both his wife and Sir Lancelot. But in the end he agreed. The next morning he went out hunting and sent word to the queen that he would be out all night. Sir Agravaine and Sir Mordred and twelve other knights who were jealous of Sir Lancelot hid in a chamber next door to the queen's chamber and waited silently for her lover to join her. Once he was inside the room, his enemies rushed to the door and cried out, "You traitor, Sir Lancelot, now you are taken! Come out of the queen's chamber!"

Sir Lancelot had no armor but his sword, but he was determined not to be taken. He wrapped his cloak tightly round his sword arm and called through the door, "Now, fair lords, leave your noise and your rushing, and I shall set open this door and then you may do with me what you like." Then he unbarred the door and opened it a crack so that only one man at a time might get through. The first

who came was Sir Colgrevance of Gore, who struck out at
Sir Lancelot with all his strength; but Lancelot deflected
the blow with his thickly wrapped arm and knocked his
opponent groveling to the floor.

"Then Sir Lancelot with great might drew the knight
within the chamber door, and with the help of the queen
and her ladies was armed in Colgrevance's armor, and set
open the chamber door and mightily strode in among the
knights. And anon, at the first stroke he slew Sir Agravaine
and anon, after, twelve of his fellows, for there was none
of the twelve knights might stand Sir Lancelot one buffet.
And also he wounded Sir Mordred, and therewithal Mordred fled with all his might . . . to King Arthur, sore
wounded and all bloodied.

" 'Ah! Jesu, mercy! How may this be?' said the king.
'Took you him in the queen's chamber?'

" 'Yea! So God me help!' said Sir Mordred, 'There we
found him.' And so he told the king from the beginning to
the ending. . . .

" 'Alas,' said the king, 'now I am sure the noble fellowship of the Round Table is broken for ever.' "

Overwhelmed with grief, Arthur gave orders that the
queen must be burned to death for treason in accordance
with the laws of England. Sir Gawain pleaded with his
uncle not to do so, but Arthur would not listen to him.
Gawain refused to be present, and the king commanded
his younger brothers, Gareth and Gaheris, to escort the
queen to the stake and witness her punishment. They were
as reluctant as Sir Gawain, but too young to disobey the
king's command. In token of their protest, however, they
insisted on attending the queen to her execution unarmed.

*A curious medieval addition to the
Arthurian legend is the notion of
a false Guinevere, an impostor
with whom Arthur lived while the
true Guinevere was banished. In
this grimly realistic scene the
impostor is about to be burned at
the stake along with a hermit but
is rescued in the nick of time, just
like the real Queen Guinevere.*

Guinevere was led to the stake, outside the city of Carlisle, and a priest heard her last confession. But just as the fire was about to be lit, Sir Lancelot and a large band of his friends galloped up, wildly lashing out with their swords, and striking to the ground all those who resisted them. "And in this rushing and hurling, as Sir Lancelot pressed hither and thither, it misfortuned him to slay Sir Gaheris and Sir Gareth," whom he did not recognize in the confusion. Then Lancelot cut Guinevere loose from her bonds and rode away with her to his castle, Joyous Garde, where his friends flocked to join him.

When news was brought to Arthur of this affray, and of the death of Gaheris and Gareth, the king fainted for pure sorrow. When he came to, he began to bewail the loss of " 'the fairest fellowship of noble knights that Christian king ever held together. Within these two days I have lost nigh forty knights and also the noble fellowship of Sir Lancelot and his blood. And the death of Sir Gaheris and Sir Gareth will cause the greatest mortal war that ever was, for I am sure that when their brother, Sir Gawain, knows thereof I shall never have rest of him till I have destroyed Sir Lancelot. And therefore, wit you well, my heart was never so

Lancelot and Guinevere part for the last time: he to go into banishment overseas, she to return to Arthur. The drawing at right, from a northern Italian prose romance compiled in 1446, shows the queen swooning gracefully in the arms of her unhappy lover, whose name is written on his hat.

The final events in Guinevere's career are depicted in two thirteenth-century French miniatures. Her spirited flight to the Tower of London resulted in its siege (above) by Mordred, seen attacking the Tower while its defenders peer forth anxiously. At right, a kneeling Guinevere seeks refuge with the nuns of Amesbury after Arthur's death. She ended her days there as the convent's abbess.

sorry as it is now. And much more am I sorrier for my good knights' loss than for the loss of my fair queen, for queens I might have enough, but such a fellowship of good knights shall never be together again.'"

King Arthur sent through all England to summon his knights, and then he laid siege to Sir Lancelot in Joyous Garde. There were many battles, but in all of them Sir Lancelot held back and would not fight his hardest, because he loved Arthur and had no heart to fight against him. At last the Pope interceded to arrange a truce by which Arthur would forgive Guinevere and take her back again. But Sir Gawain would not allow the king to forgive Sir Lancelot. Thus Lancelot was banished to his kingdom of Benwick in France, and King Arthur and Sir Gawain crossed the Channel with sixty thousand men to make war on him there.

In Arthur's absence Mordred, who had been appointed regent of England and guardian of Queen Guinevere, seized his chance to replace his father on the throne. He pretended that he had received a letter announcing King Arthur's death, and with that excuse, he called a parliament and had himself chosen king and crowned at Canterbury. Then he rode to Winchester and told Guinevere that since her husband was dead, he would marry her himself.

But Queen Guinevere fled away to London and took the Tower of London, "and suddenly in all haste possible she stuffed it with all manner of victual, and well garnished it with men, and so kept it. Then Sir Mordred was passing wroth out of measure. And a short tale for to make, he went and laid a mighty siege about the Tower of London, and made many great assaults, and threw many great engines unto them and shot great guns."

When news came that Arthur was returning home to be avenged, however, Sir Mordred had to lift the siege and make for Dover to oppose the landing of his father's troops. At Dover "there was much slaughter of gentle knights and many a bold baron was laid full low." But both Arthur and Mordred survived to fight again another day; and on that day there was "never seen a more dolefuller battle in no Christian land." From morning until night the fighting raged, until a hundred thousand noble knights lay dead upon the field. "Then was King Arthur wroth out of measure when he saw his people so slain, and he looked about him and was aware where stood Sir Mordred leaning upon his sword among a great heap of dead men."

MS. XX FOL. 163 V: ROYAL LIBRARY, THE HAGUE

Arthur's last battle with Mordred was one he had tried to avoid. But a truce agreed on by the two armies was broken when a knight saw a snake at his feet and drew his sword to kill it. This was the signal for a bloody onslaught, pic-

Gripping his spear in both hands, he ran upon Mordred, crying out, "Traitor! Now is thy death day come!" With all his force he plunged his spear into Mordred's stomach beneath the shield, and its point passed right through Mordred's body and came bursting out of his back. But with his death's wound upon him, Mordred raised his sword and struck his father so ferocious a blow upon the helmet that the steel edge cut through the visor and entered Arthur's skull.

"And noble Arthur fell in a swoon to the earth, and there he swooned oftentimes." Sir Bedivere, the last of his knights still left alive, although he, too, was grievously wounded, knelt down and held the king in his arms.

tured here in a Dutch manuscript made in the early 1300's. At left, Mordred is literally sliced apart by Arthur as he simultaneously gives his father his deathblow. At right the stricken king is carried from the battlefield in a cart.

A thirteenth-century artist's rendering (left) of the famous moment when Bedivere, after hesitating twice, finally throws Excalibur into the lake shows a monstrous arm brandishing the sword while King Arthur sits miserably in the foreground. At right, the death of Arthur is portrayed in romantic fashion in a drawing made by Rossetti in 1857. Eight mourning queens are grouped around the prostrate king, while in the background a ship waits to transport him to Avalon.

"My time passes fast, Sir Bedivere," King Arthur said. "Take my good sword, Excalibur, and go with it to yonder water's side and throw it into the water."

Sir Bedivere went to the lake nearby and hurled Excalibur as far across the water as he could; and as it fell, a hand came up to grasp it by the handle, to wave it three times in farewell, before taking it down into the deep. Then Sir Bedivere took the king upon his back and carried him down to the water's edge. Here stood a little barge in which sat many fair ladies wearing black veils and weeping bitterly.

"Now put me into that barge," said King Arthur, "For I must go into the vale of Avalon to heal me of my grievous wound. And if thou hear nevermore of me, pray for my soul." Sir Bedivere had put the king down gently, laying his head upon the lap of one of the ladies, and the barge sailed away into the mists, and King Arthur was heard of no more.

"Yet some men say in many parts of England King Arthur is not dead but had by the will of our Lord Jesus into another place. And men say that he shall come again and he shall win the Holy Cross. And many men say that there is written upon the tomb this:

HIC IACET ARTHURUS, REX QUONDAM REXQUE FUTURUS
Here lies King Arthur, the Once and Future King"

Such is the theme of Malory's story, and such its atmos-

phere. Based on earlier French romances, which were themselves based on Geoffrey of Monmouth's *History of the Kings of Britain*, which, in turn, was based on who knows what earlier records, legends, and oral traditions, it has taken us a long way from the harsh reality of the fifth century and from the threatened island of Britain in which the real Arthur was born.

THE THREATENED ISLAND

The fifth century witnessed the disintegration of the Roman Empire. For years Rome had been striving to defend its far-flung frontiers, which stretched some 10,000 miles, from the North Sea along the Rhine and across to the Danube, and so to the shores of the Black Sea; and from Constantinople right around the Mediterranean to the Strait of Gibraltar, then northward through Spain and Gaul—Roman provinces for centuries—to Britain, the island that marked Rome's farthest expansion to the northwest. But the once-civilized Roman way of life had become sterile and decadent; Rome's emperors were men of little importance, puppets in the hands of their generals, who frequently assassinated them and took their places on the throne. The superb administration that had enabled the government in Rome to keep control of an unwieldy conglomeration of nations and provinces had degenerated into a bureaucracy riddled with corruption. Trade declined as taxes increased. The Roman army, once so proud of its legions of well-equipped soldiers, more and more consisted of troops of barbarians, hired to defend the empire against steadily increasing pressure from other bands of barbarians—Goths, Vandals, Saxons, Huns—moving southward and westward from Scandinavia, the lands around the Baltic, and the distant Russian steppes.

In 429, under the leadership of their cunning and ruthless King Gaiseric, a horde of Vandals poured out of Spain and into Roman Africa, the main source of Rome's corn supply and the home of a prosperous civilization. They made their way along the North African coast, conquering and pillaging as they went, and in 439 they captured Carthage, Rome's great African seaport. Gaiseric ordered

Built in the second century to defend the Roman province of Britain against attack by the Picts, Hadrian's Wall still sprawls across a countryside of cliffs and bracken-covered moors that has changed little since Arthur's day.

the building of a great pirate fleet, and using Carthage as their base, the Vandals began to ravage the Roman cities around the Mediterranean Sea and even to threaten Rome itself.

Already endangered by barbarian pressure along its northern and eastern frontiers, Rome no longer could offer any protection to the distant island of Britain. One legion after another was called back to fight Rome's wars on the Continent, until only a small regular garrison remained. By 410, most of that had been withdrawn, and although there may have been a brief decade of reoccupation between 417 and 429, by the middle of the century, Roman power effectively had ended. The islanders were left to fend for themselves.

For almost a century already, Roman Britain had been under intermittent attack. From the north there was constant raiding by fierce, tattooed Pictish tribesmen, who came down from the Caledonian mountains of Scotland. In the second century A.D. the Emperor Hadrian had built a great wall across the country from east to west between the River Tyne and the Solway Firth, to keep the Picts out of the Romanized country farther south. But once the legions that had defended it with their lives were gone, the Picts clambered over the abandoned ramparts and swarmed south toward the Humber. The Picts were followed by the Scotti, marauders from Ireland, who sailed across the Irish Sea in their light skin-and-wood boats called curraghs. They pillaged wherever they landed on the western coasts of England and Wales, terrifying the fishermen and farmers, spearing and knifing those who could not escape, and setting fire to their thatched-roof huts. Far worse a threat than either the Picts or the Irish warbands, however, was the growing power of the Saxons, users of the *seax* or short-sword, and their northern neighbors the Angles and the Jutes, who fished and farmed in what is now southern Denmark.

The Angles, Jutes, and Saxons were expanding nations that no longer were content with their restricted farmlands on the Continental mainland. As Roman power declined in Britain, they had begun to look west for more land on which to settle, a rich land that had been a Roman province for more than three hundred years, where there would be plenty of plunder and a good life for all. They came across the North Sea in long, shallow-draught galleys roughly constructed of overlapping oak planks, curved up at either end, and rowed by a score of sturdy warriors. They were a fair

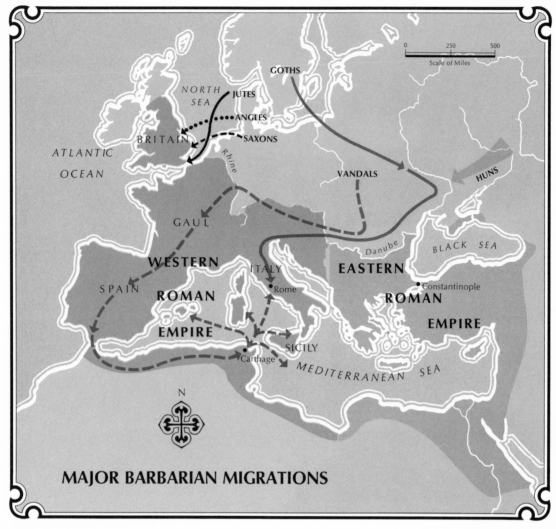

MAJOR BARBARIAN MIGRATIONS

people with long hair and beards, clothed in thick, coarse shirts and trousers, in cloaks to which skins were sewn by their women so as to give them extra warmth when they were used as blankets at night. As well as their short-swords, they carried thick, iron-spiked spears, battle-axes, and round wooden shields covered with hide. Few of them wore helmets; fewer still wore coats of ring mail, which cost good money from the armorers of the Rhineland. Even among the leaders there were some who did not even have a thick leather jerkin to protect them. But they were ruthless, violent men who exulted in their animal energy, and all along the southern and eastern coasts of Britain they pillaged and looted, raped and murdered, burning the farms, killing the livestock, and then sailing home.

The barbarian migrations shown here penetrated the Western Roman Empire between the fourth and sixth centuries and effectively brought about its downfall.

OVERLEAF: *Roman London, an impressive walled city that was also a thriving port, is reconstructed in a modern painting. The city is viewed from the southeast. A trestle bridge spans the Thames on the site where London Bridge afterward would stand; the Basilica, the largest building in the city, is seen at center right.*

THE LONDON MUSEUM

61

Roman influences on Britain were strong and long-lasting. Like the citizens of other provinces, the British paid heavy taxes (left, above), which helped to maintain the empire. The Roman fondness for bathing resulted in a British spa, built over the hot springs at Bath. The Roman baths there (right, above) exist to this day.

Late-fourth-century Britain was still one of the most pleasant provinces of the western Roman Empire, though no longer so prosperous as it had been. The rolling downs and plains of the south and west were dotted with the stucco-and-brick villas of gentlemen-farmers—although many had been abandoned and now stood empty, their brightly painted walls already crumbling into ruins and the pinkish tiles beginning to fall from their roofs. In winter the well-furnished rooms of these villas had been warmed by heated flues that ran beneath their mosaic floors; in summer fountains used to play in the courtyards and grapevines grew against the garden walls. Outside their gates good, straight roads still led to the towns that had been Rome's chief contribution to the British way of life—towns whose paved streets and imposing buildings were constructed in the regular, rectilinear manner favored by the architects of Rome.

Roads intersected the island, linking northern fortress with southern port, garrison with tribal capital, stretching from the forts along Hadrian's Wall to the clustered villas of the South Downs, from the legionary fortress at Chester in the west to the large town of Caistor-next-Norwich on the east coast. And at the center of this complex of roads stood Londinium, one of the most impressive cities north of the Alps.

Roman London was a city of some 30,000 inhabitants, living in an area of over three hundred acres enclosed by three miles of strong stone walls, nine feet thick, up to twenty feet high, and pierced by gates where the main roads led through them. The river gate, which faced the traveler

The Roman custom of serving food attractively led to the establishment of British potteries, which produced fine lusterware, such as the beaker below, decorated with a relief of chariot racing. Rich households treasured silver plate like this magnificent dish, buried during the Saxon invasions and found during World War II.

as he came across the wide wooden bridge spanning the Thames, opened onto the street leading up to the Basilica, which was the center of commerce and government, a vast and impressive building, more than 420 feet long, with high arcaded walls. Just inside this river gate were the public baths, and other bathhouses were dotted all over the city. Down the streets on either side as far as the eye could see were the wide, arched fronts of the numerous shops and countinghouses and the porticoed homes of the prosperous merchants.

Life in Londinium, like life in the other big towns of Roman Britain, was well organized and pleasant for all but the poor and the slaves who did the heavy work. The farms outside the walls, and the gardens within them, produced fine meat, vegetables, and fruit; fresh, clear water, piped in hollowed tree trunks, was plentiful; the Thames, at whose wharves were moored scores of trading ships, was full of salmon and trout and shoals of fresh-water fish. There was no shortage of work. There were brickfields, potteries, and glassworks, joiners' shops and mills, masons' yards and furniture factories, as well as row upon row of warehouses and worksheds along the river front. Latin was the universal language, written as well as spoken. The civilized citizens of Londinium were a far cry from the savage Ger-

manic pirates and raiders from across the sea—barbarians who worshiped gods of war, who feared and hated towns as unfamiliar places where evil spirits dwelt, whose idea of luxury was an encampment under the stars and a bellyful of meat and spruce beer.

The Britons, Romanized and peaceable, were no match for such men. Although they still were held together by strong tribal loyalties and tribal customs, particularly so in the more remote areas of the island, they no longer were possessed of that warlike spirit that had fired the hearts of the Iceni tribe when they followed their Queen Boudicca into battle against the Roman conquerors long ago in the reign of the Emperor Nero. Accustomed for centuries to relying on the empire's legions to protect them, the Britons now were incapable of protecting themselves, and as the fourth century drew to its close, they grew ever more in need of protection.

The Saxons, an increasing menace, now had established settled bases along the Continental coast from which Britain could be raided more easily. In the west the Scotti from Ireland were becoming ever more threatening under their powerful High King Niall of the Nine Hostages. Repeated raids were made along the coasts that faced the turbulent Irish Sea, and prisoners were carried off in hundreds to become the slaves of Irish chieftains. King Niall's pirates thrust as far inland as Chester, Caerleon-on-Usk, and Wroxeter, and although in 405 King Niall himself was killed at sea, the raids did not stop.

Yet even after the legions had gone and the Vandals had begun to swarm across Roman Africa under King Gaiseric, Roman Britain had not lost all hope of survival. In 429 there arrived in the island a bishop from Auxerre in Gaul, a bishop named Germanus, who had been a soldier in his youth and never had lost his taste for battle. Bishop Germanus found Britain a "most wealthy island," with still-thriving communities governed by local kings whose families had been used to kingship from ancient times. Even before the Romans occupied Britain permanently in A.D. 43, Cunobelinus, the original of Shakespeare's Cymbeline, the powerful ruler of the Catuvellauni tribe in southern Britain, used to style himself *rex*, or king, on the coins issued from his

A map of Britain in the late fifth and early sixth centuries identifies the sites mentioned in chapters III and IV, gives tentative locations for five Arthurian battles, and shows the extent of Saxon encroachment.

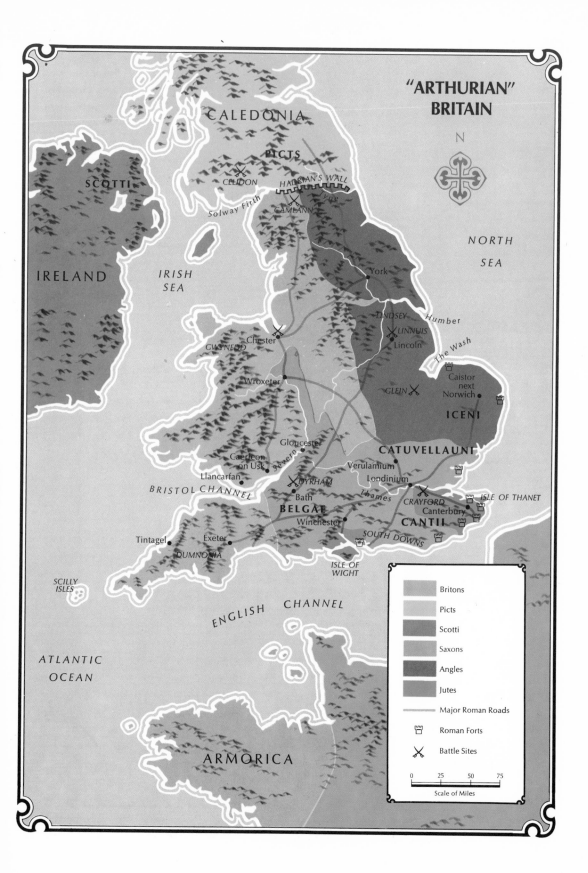

"ARTHURIAN" BRITAIN

N

CALEDONIA

PICTS

SCOTTI

CELIDON

HADRIAN'S WALL

Solway Firth

CAMLANN

Tyne

IRELAND

IRISH SEA

NORTH SEA

York

LINDSEY

Humber

Chester

LINNUIS

GWYNEDD

Lincoln

The Wash

Wroxeter

Caistor next Norwich

GLEIN

ICENI

Gloucester

Caerleon on Usk

Severn

Verulanium

CATUVELLAUNI

Llancarfan

DYRHAM

Londinium

BRISTOL CHANNEL

Bath

Thames

BELGAE

Winchester

CRAYFORD

ISLE OF THANET

Canterbury

Tintagel

Exeter

CANTII

SOUTH DOWNS

DUMNONIA

ISLE OF WIGHT

SCILLY ISLES

ENGLISH CHANNEL

ATLANTIC OCEAN

Britons
Picts
Scotti
Saxons
Angles
Jutes

———— Major Roman Roads

Roman Forts

Battle Sites

ARMORICA

0   25   50   75

Scale of Miles

Roman engineering skill made possible the construction of fortresses that seemed impregnable to barbarian warriors who did not understand siege warfare. The besiegers in this second-century relief are Dacians; later, far to the west, similar scenes were repeated as Saxon invaders swarmed around the Roman-built walls of British towns. By Arthur's time, however, they had battered their way into most of the towns in eastern Britain and had celebrated afterward by drinking from richly enameled horns like the one at right.

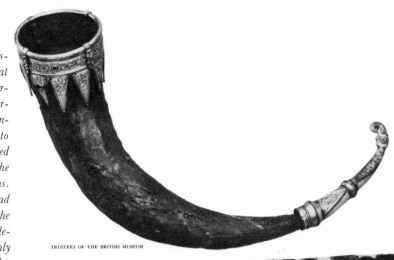

mint. With the breakdown of Roman rule, the Britons were tending more and more to honor the ancient ties and rally around their regional leaders.

Despite the constant inroads by the barbarians, Germanus found that town life still was going on. Trade in the port of Londinium remained active; in Verulamium, farther north, the Roman theater had become a refuse dump for the decaying vegetables of the market, but the shops still were open and local crafts still flourished. Germanus also found that while the invaders might destroy isolated farms near the coast, burn down the wattle-and-daub huts of peasants and the timber hovels of fishermen, trample down crops and orchards, vineyards and gardens, they were not yet capable of fighting a pitched battle or of storming the masonry walls of a Roman town or fort.

Before his arrival in Britain Germanus had been military governor of the Armorican district of Gaul, with responsibility for guarding the Channel coast. Yet it was not as a soldier that he had been sent to Britain, but as a preacher who could combat a new heresy called Pelagianism. A Briton named Pelagius had begun to teach that the soul is born in a neutral condition and that the human will was perfectly free to make its own choice between virtue and vice. This idea denied the whole concept of original sin, and the pious bishops of Rome feared that such a teaching might undermine the authority of the Church. Germanus, however, was as concerned with the bodies of the British people as with their souls.

He reorganized the bands of local militia, persuaded their leaders to appoint him their supreme commander, or *dux*, and taught them how to fight a formal battle. When next the barbarians appeared, the Britons were better prepared to meet them. Instead of retreating inland in panic, driven like sheep before the advancing Saxons, terrified by the shouts of the savage throng and the braying of their war horns, they withdrew in good order, drawing their oppressors into the trap that Germanus had laid for them. The Saxons marched on, unsuspecting, into a narrow valley, and when they had gone too far to retreat out of the bottleneck, Germanus broke his wary silence. Rising to his feet, he cried out at the top of his voice, "Alleluia!" The waiting Britons took up the cry, and to repeated shouts of "Alleluia! Alleluia!" they rushed down both sides of the valley onto their trapped enemies. The Saxons, surprised and alarmed by this unexpected reply to their own war cries, turned on their heels and fled, dropping their spears as they ran.

TRAJAN'S COLUMN, ROME: ALINARI

It was a great victory, but only a temporary respite. The years passed, and the Saxons and their allies grew more resolute and more enterprising. They came now not only in galleys but also in ships with leather sails, leaving their vessels concealed in coastal inlets, advancing down the neglected roads, driving ever deeper into the British countryside. They became expert at besieging and storming fortified encampments, at recognizing the weak link in a chain of defenses and battering their way through it. Soon they began to settle down on the land they formerly had been content to pillage and lay waste, and they established small farming settlements of rough huts around the wooden halls of their thanes, or lords.

In 446 the Britons made a final, forlorn plea for help from Rome. Those parts of Romanized Britain that still were able to act collectively joined in dispatching an urgent message to Aetius, the Roman general in Gaul:

To Aetius, three times consul, the groans of the Britons; the barbarians drive us to the sea, the sea drives us to the barbarians; between these two forms of death, we are either massacred or drowned.

Medieval English chroniclers copied Geoffrey of Monmouth in making Vortigern a villain. His betrayal of Britain to the Saxons led to his death at the hands of Ambrosius, who was inflamed by his treachery. Above, Vortigern is burned in a tower where he had sought refuge from Ambrosius.

But there was no response; Aetius had enough to do fending off barbarian inroads in Gaul itself. No help came.

Then—or so it seems from the confused and incomplete records of these times—a call was made to a leader closer to home, to Vortigern, a powerful British ruler who had gained control of an extensive district in the west of Britain and who exercised a considerable influence over the south of the island as well. According to some sources, Vortigern is supposed to have married Sevira, daughter of the Roman Emperor Maximus, and thus, though a rough and ready British-speaking overlord himself, he had some respect for Roman ways. His advice to the Britons was to bring a Roman solution to bear upon Britain's problems.

The Roman Empire had relied for the maintenance of its power not only upon recruits taken into its army from all the world's races, but also upon whole tribes, enlisted to defend particular areas. These tribes were known as *foederati*, because they had entered into a *foedus*, or treaty, with Rome; its terms usually were that they would be admitted into the empire in return for defending whatever portion of it they were allotted, and although the soldiers thus gained land within the empire, they maintained their own laws and customs and their own identities. This policy, Vortigern apparently suggested—and the British councilors

agreed—should be adopted now. In return for their help in keeping at bay the Picts and Scotti and any other raiders, and on the understanding that they live at peace with their British neighbors, a war band of Saxon troops and their women were accepted and settled in the southeastern region of Britain.

According to the Venerable Bede, the Northumbrian monk and historian whose *History of the English Church and People,* completed in 731, is our chief source of knowledge for this period, the leaders of the federated troops were two Jutish chiefs, named Hengist and Horsa. They established themselves on the Isle of Thanet, an area of rich farmland separated from Kent (the land of the Cantii tribe) by a nar-

Ambrosius hated Vortigern because the tyrant had arranged the murder of Britain's King Constans, Ambrosius' brother, in order to seize the throne himself. A Byzantine influence is evident in this fourteenth-century Italian miniature, in which Vortigern, now king (at right), orders the execution of the men he had hired to kill his predecessor. A team of horses drags them away to their deaths.

71

row channel, which was guarded at each end by a Roman fort. This was a long way distant from the areas of Britain under attack by the Picts and the Irish warbands, but it was convenient for Vortigern to keep them under his control when they were not fighting in the north, and the Saxon federates were well placed to undertake coastal patrols for the protection of Londinium.

Although they were brutal fighters, the Saxons had an impressive artistic and linguistic culture. The bust of a Germanic warrior at left —obviously modeled from life— shows a youth with an unusually strong face. Descendants of these Saxon invaders left England an indelible legacy, the language on which modern English is based.

LANDESMUSEUM, TRIER

At first all went well. The Picts and Scotti were sub-dued; the Kentish settlement prospered; and Britain enjoyed a period of unaccustomed peace. But gradually the settlers called over friends and reinforcements—Angles, Jutes, and Saxons—from across the North Sea and began spreading themselves ever deeper into southeastern Britain. They demanded more and more land and more generous payments. At some time in the 450's the increasingly angry quarrels between them and their British employers flared into open war. In 457 there was a ferocious battle at Crayford in Kent, and the Britons, having lost four thousand men on the field, "fled to London in great terror."

This is the last recorded mention of London for a century and a half; Britain's capital and other Roman towns in turn fell victim to the invaders, now armed with the Roman siege equipment that had fallen into their hands. The Saxons advanced farther and farther inland, devastating countryside and towns alike:

Public and private buildings were razed [according to Bede], priests were slain at the altar; bishops and people alike, regardless of rank, were destroyed with fire and sword, and none remained to bury those who had suffered a cruel death. A few wretched survivors captured in the hills were butchered wholesale, and others, desperate with hunger, came out and surrendered to the enemy for food, although they were doomed to lifelong slavery even if they escaped instant massacre. Some fled overseas in their misery; others, clinging to their homeland, eked out a wretched and fearful existence.

Bede's picture is a fearful one, yet the vast majority of survivors probably stayed close to what once had been their homes, in great discomfort and misery. Some may have sailed across the Channel to the old Roman province of Armorica, the first stage of three centuries of migration that eventually took a British (Celtic) language—and gave the modern name of Brittany—to this great Atlantic peninsula.

It was fortunate, then, that in the West Country there was a tribal leader strong enough to make a stand against the Saxon menace and to offer shelter to those who had escaped its shadow or were prepared to take up arms in defense of the old culture. This man's name was Ambrosius, a ruler who seems to have advised Vortigern of the dangers of the Saxon alliance and to have managed to stand aloof from its consequences.

Ambrosius apparently was of Roman descent. The land over which he ruled was certainly as Romanized as any in

TEXT CONTINUED ON PAGE 76

GAWAIN: CHILD OF THE SUN

Many of the attributes of Gawain—the most genuinely British of Arthur's many knights—are those of an ancient Celtic hero, Cuchullin, offspring of the sun god. Gawain's own connection with the sun is revealed in his name, which means "bright-haired" in Welsh, and in the fact that his strength waxed until noon and then waned with the setting sun. Gawain—whose shield was emblazoned with a lion, above—frequently was involved with women on his quests. In the German manuscript at right, made about 1460, Gawain, staying overnight in a Castle of Ladies, finds himself on a Perilous Bed, being assailed by an incredible variety of weapons. In an English poem, "Sir Gawain and the Green Knight," Gawain impetuously accepts the challenge of a green knight by beheading him in Arthur's hall. Magically, the head speaks (above, left), claiming the right to take a similar stroke at Gawain. Later, Gawain visits a castle and virtuously resists an attempt by his host's wife to seduce him (left); her husband turns out to be the Green Knight.

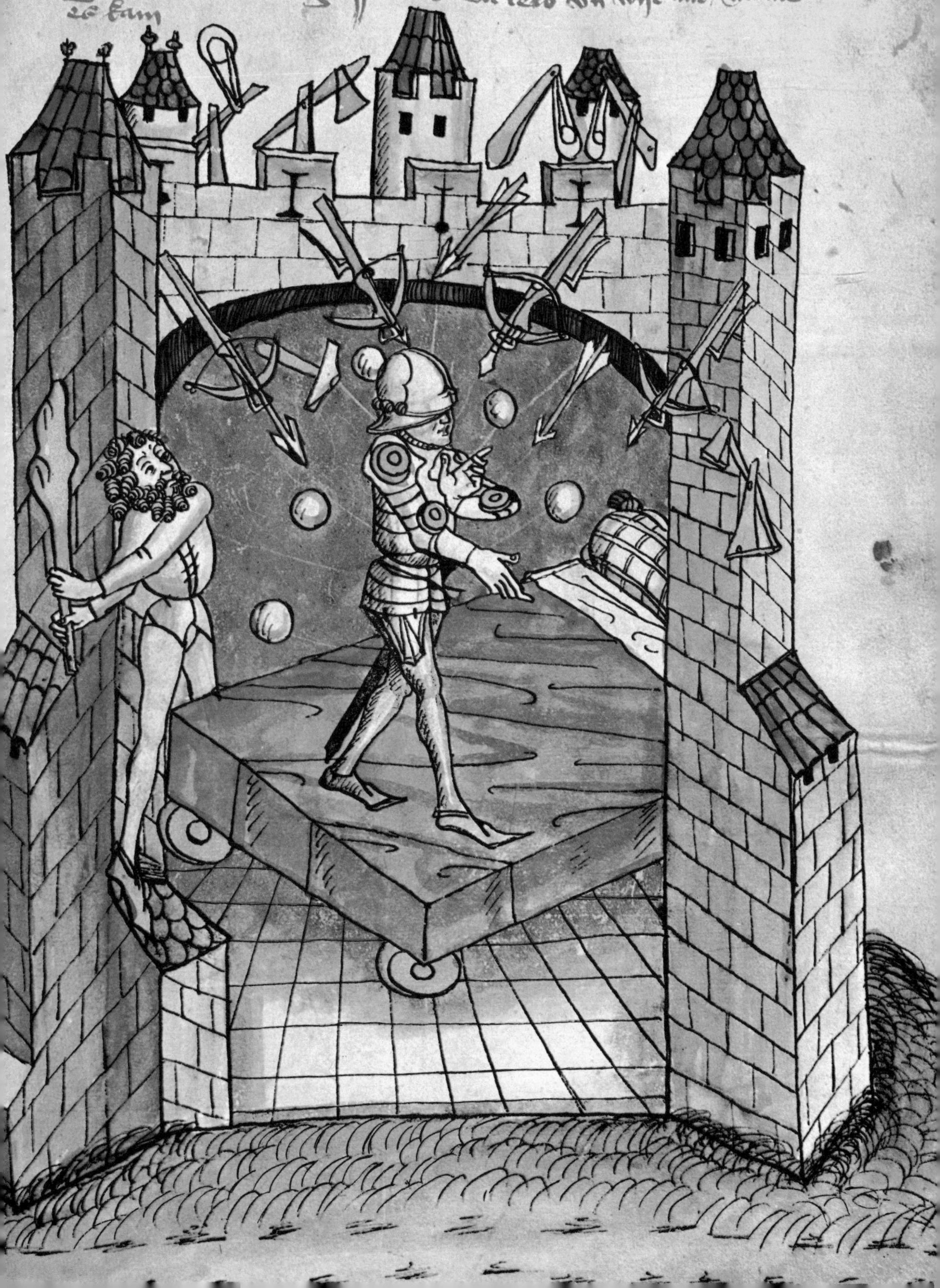

TEXT CONTINUED FROM PAGE 73

Britain and probably remained so, even at this time, preserving what it could of the traditions of Roman culture and organizing both its government and its army on the Roman model. Although the Saxon warrior Aelle landed near Selsey in 477 and carved out for himself the kingdom of the South Saxons (which has given its name to the present-day county of Sussex), and although in 495 Cerdic landed on the shore of Southampton Water to found the kingdom of the West Saxons (which later would become King Alfred's kingdom of Wessex), farther to the west the Romano-British kingdom of Ambrosius remained secure. To this haven, says the earliest of British historians, a monk

The Venerable Bede, whose History of the English Church and People *was completed in 731, works at his writing table.*

named Gildas, writing in the sixth century, men from the other threatened tribes of Britain flocked "as eagerly as bees when a storm is brewing."

For the time being, Ambrosius prevented the storm from breaking over his kingdom. A contemporary writer on the Continent described Britain in the 480's as being prosperous and peaceful despite the Saxon incursions. By 500, there was a considerable settlement of Saxons along the east coast (Essex), and the kingdoms of Sussex and Wessex continued to flourish and expand. Yet in the Cotswold Hills, along the borders of Wales, and in Dumnonia (the peninsula occupied today by the counties of Devon and Cornwall) Roman Britain contrived to live on.

Both written records and archaeological evidence for even the most superficial history of Britain at this time are tantalizingly sparse. Nevertheless, it is possible to build a credible picture, from what few materials do exist, of what life probably was like in the western area of Britain loyal to Ambrosius.

Some sort of seaborne trade was maintained with such Atlantic ports as Bordeaux and Nantes and with the Mediterranean—increasingly so after about 500. Small amounts

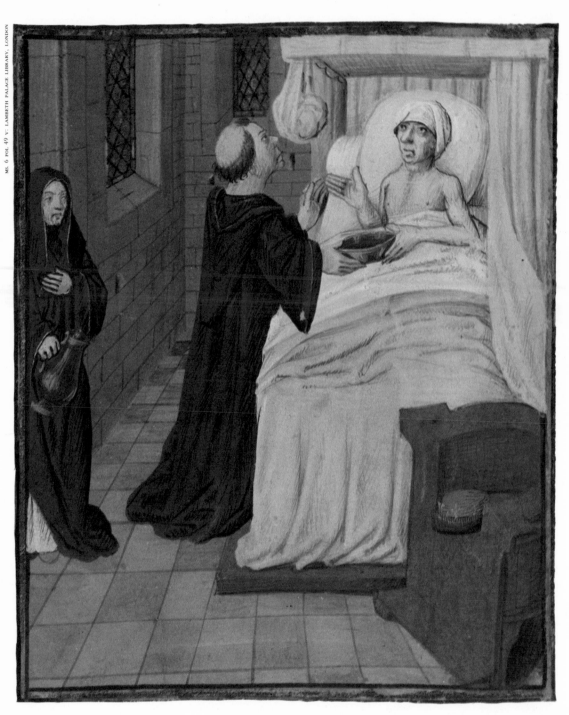

A fifteenth-century illustration depicts Ambrosius' death. The pious-looking monk offering the sick man a drink is actually a Saxon in Vortigern's pay, and the bowl contains poison, which will kill the king in his sleep.

of wine, in pottery amphoras (jars), and perhaps cooking oil as well, came in the ships of the traders. Early writings suggest that corn, woolen goods, and hides, perhaps Irish wolfhounds (which evidently were highly prized for their speed and strength), and perhaps even slaves, were exported in return.

In a few centers like Gloucester, life may have been carried on in the old Roman way, with Latin still the language of a household proud of its links with the past, treasuring its manuscripts, its silver and pewter tableware, its civilized methods of worship—whether the belief was in Christ or in some pagan gods.

But in most of Ambrosius' kingdom people had reverted to a less Romanized way of life, grouped together in small communities like the hill forts of their ancestors, using native pottery that was made by hand—not thrown on the wheel like the Roman ware—and speaking a variety of British dialects. For the poor, as always, life was hard. Living in huts of stone and thatch, laboriously tilling their small square fields, attempting to improve their plain diet of bread and occasional pieces of meat with strong herbs, dressed in rough woolen clothes, such people would have had little cause to celebrate the pleasures of human existence. Yet they valued their freedom and their sense of national identity—and they were prepared to fight for them.

Perhaps to protect themselves against Saxon invasion, possibly to protect their cattle from raids, either by the Saxons or by other British tribes, the inhabitants of this last enclave of Romano-British civilization threw up a series of linear earthworks. One of the largest of these is known today as the Wansdyke, a huge man-made ridge that stretches fifty miles from Inkpen in what is now Berkshire, across Savernake Forest and the Marlborough Downs, over a Roman road that used to lead into Bath, and on down toward the Bristol Channel. Historians are uncertain of its purpose, but its presence, rising up from the peaceful fields of the modern English countryside, is a reminder of some tremendous joint effort by people who can have had only the most primitive implements to aid them.

Under Ambrosius the Britons suffered setbacks and defeats, but they won victories, too. They may have lost ground occasionally, but they never were driven into serious retreat. They had a cause and they had a leader. Yet men were bound to wonder what would happen when that leader died, as he was bound to. Could anyone replace Ambrosius? Could any man be a more memorable leader?

With their warrior king dead, the Britons' desperate need for a leader in their struggle against the Saxons was answered by a young man whose ability would make him into a legend—Arthur.

IV

"COMMANDER IN THE BATTLES"

In those days [that followed the death of Ambrosius] the Saxons grew in numbers and prospered in Britain. . . . Then Arthur the warrior and the kings of the Britons fought against the Saxons, but Arthur himself was the *dux bellorum*, the commander in the battles. The first battle was on the mouth of the river which is called Glein. The second, the third, the fourth, and the fifth upon another river, which is called Dubglass, and is in the region of Linnuis. The sixth battle was upon the river which is called Bassas.

The seventh battle was in the wood of Celidon, that is Cat Coit Celidon. The eighth was the battle by the castle of Guinnion, in which Arthur carried upon his shoulders an image of the Blessed Mary, the Eternal Virgin. And the heathen were turned to flight on that day, and great was the slaughter brought upon them through the virtue of our Lord, Jesus Christ, and through the virtue of the Blessed Virgin, His Mother.

On a box lid made of whalebone a seventh-century Anglo-Saxon carved an intricately detailed scene of his countrymen at war. At right, a castle's defenders shower arrows on a group of attackers, who protect themselves by holding up their shields. Below the circle in the center, where the handle of the box was attached, a woman weeps over the body of a warrior.

The ninth battle was fought in the City of the Legion. The tenth battle was waged on the banks of the river which is called Tribruit. The eleventh battle was fought in the mountain which is called Agned. The twelfth battle was on Mount Badon where in one day nine hundred and sixty men fell in one onslaught of Arthur's. And no one laid them low but himself alone. And in all these battles he stood out as victor.

Thus Arthur makes his first appearance in a historical chronicle. Its compiler was the Welsh monk Nennius, who was writing in the ninth century; the work is the same *Historia Brittonum* that relates the "marvels" of the stone that bears the footprint of Arthur's dog Cabal and of the mysterious mound that marks the grave of Arthur's son Anir.

But although these marvels may defy belief, Nennius is more credible when he comes to this list of twelve victories won by Arthur as commander of the British forces. For while some of the places named by Nennius no longer are identifiable, some guesses have been made as to the location of the others, based on the ninth-century Welsh form of the place names. It is impossible now to identify the sites of Castle Guinnion, the mountain called Agned, or the River Bassas, but it has been assumed that the region of Linnuis could be the Lindsey area of Lincolnshire south of the Humber and that the River Glein is the Lincolnshire River Glen. This certainly would support the belief that Arthur may have been called upon to campaign against the Saxons and Angles who were landing in increasing numbers on the east coast of Britain in the early sixth century—giving their name to the area now known as East Anglia. The wood of Celidon probably is the forest of Caledonia in the wild Scottish uplands beyond Hadrian's Wall, where a campaign against the Picts was fought at about this time. The City of the Legion probably is Chester. Mount Badon has been variously identified with Badbury near Swindon in Wiltshire, Badbury Hill in Berkshire, Badbury Rings near Blandford in Dorset, and Bedwyn near Inkpen—but in any case, it is believed to be somewhere in southern Britain in the neighborhood of the Wansdyke. Wherever it was, Mount Badon obviously must have been the site of a battle or siege of supreme importance. We may picture Arthur's troops surrounding the steep and strongly fortified hill, cutting off the supplies from the enemy who occupied it, forcing them to break out, and then slaughtering them as they tried to escape.

Because the list of battles appears to range so widely across the country, some historians have held it to be sus-

Travel and fighting were performed mostly on foot in fifth- and sixth-century Britain. Some Britons copied the Romans in wearing sandals like this one, with metal studs in the soles to make them sturdier. Others wore shoes that were shaped like ankle boots.

Morcuo duc hengisto octha fili'ci'cransi uit de sinistrali parte britcayinic ad reg nu cancoru. & de ipso orasregescancor. unc arthur pugnabat contra illos. millisdieb; cu regib; bricconu. s. ipse dux erat bellorū. Primū bellū fuit in ostiū flumi nis quod dicit glein. secdin. & tciu & qr tū & quintu. sup aliud flumen. quod dicit dubglas. in regione linnuis. Sextū bellum sup flumen quod uocat e bassas. Septimū fuit bellū in silua celidonis. id: cac coit celidon. Octauum fuit bellū in castello guinni on. Inquo arthur portauit imagine sce marie ppetue uirginis sup humeros suos. & pagani uersi s infugā in illo die. & cedes magna fuit sup illos. p uirtutem dni nri ihu xpi & p uirtutē sce marie uirginis genitricis ei. Nonu bellū gestū; in urbe legionis. Decimū gessit bellū in litore Fluminis quod uocat tribruit. Undecimū facciū bellū in monte qui dicit agned. Duo decimū fuit bellū in monte badonis inquo corruer in uno die n genti sexa ginta uiri de uno impetū arthur.

Six manuscripts of Nennius' ninth-century Historia Brittonum *still are extant; this page, from a copy of the original Latin text made around 1100, gives the account of Arthur's twelve famous battles that is quoted on page 81.*

pect, believing that it is more likely that the battles all took place in one area, the north, for instance, or the southwest. But if they ranged all over Britain, this would bear out the belief that Arthur was indeed the supreme military leader that Nennius' description of a *dux bellorum* implies—that he took his army from river to river and from coast to coast to fight the invaders whenever and wherever they seemed most threatening.

The suggestion has been made that Arthur's defense of Britain may have been conducted on the basis of a system developed by the Romans in the previous century, when the island was divided into four smaller provinces and its military organization into three commands. The Dux Britanniarum (the duke of the Britains), who had his headquarters at York, was responsible for defending the northern frontier against the Picts and Scotti; the Comes Litoris Saxonici (the count of the Saxon Shore) defended the southeastern

coast from the Germanic pirates aided by a well-built and strongly garrisoned series of forts that stretched from the Wash to the Isle of Wight. Both these leaders commanded a local militia of garrison troops, and their duties essentially were to hold the frontier line. The third leader, the Comes Britanniarum (the count of the Britains) was entrusted with the direction of a field army of six cavalry and three infantry units, an army that was mobile, able to come to the defense of his colleagues when the need arose.

It is significant that the army under the count's command was composed chiefly of cavalry. The Roman army, in its early days, had made little use of cavalry, preferring to rely on the superb discipline and fighting strength of its infantry, grouped in legions some six thousand strong. Gradually, however, as the Roman generals came in contact with barbarian troops using cavalry armed with bows and spears, they had begun to incorporate cavalry into their own commands. Usually these were lightly armed auxiliary units, made up of *foederati* fighting under the eagles, but also there were mailed cavalry, known as *cataphracti* or *clibanarii*. The cataphracts, whose name comes from a Greek word meaning "covered in mail," wore helmets and body armor made of iron scales or chain mail, with arm- and leg-pieces attached to it. The *clibanarii*, so called from the Latin word for "baking pan," were armed from head to foot in scales or mail, and their horses, too, wore protective trappings of iron scales sewn on blankets— a heavy and cumbersome uniform, especially in hot weather. Both types of cavalry were armed with long, heavy spears and swords, and they could slash their way through poorly organized enemy troops with terrible effect.

As the responsibility of defending Rome's frontiers came to demand a more flexible type of army, the Roman legions had been reorganized into smaller units, of about one thousand men to a legion, while the cavalry became a separate arm of the service. Essentially, the need was for mobility, so that the troops could be thrown into action speedily where they were needed most.

The situation in Britain also was one that demanded mobility, and it has been suggested plausibly that Arthur

The well-disciplined Roman cavalry, clad in mail and armed with spears and shields, as shown at left, may have been the model for Arthur's horsemen. This relief commemorates a Roman campaign against German tribesmen between 177 and 180, when the barbarians still could be subdued by such brutal means as the systematic beheading of prisoners (foreground).

served in some capacity resembling that of a count of the Britains, deploying a small force of cavalry, which may or may not have been armored, but which, like its Roman predecessors, was professionally disciplined and extremely effective in dealing with Saxon foes who had no horses and who fought with great bravery but little organization.

As commander in chief, then, ranging far and wide with his band of "knights," Arthur would have been directing a campaign on whose success the whole of Britain's freedom and future depended. He would have been the one man capable of organizing the island's defense against the heathen invaders, the one leader capable of inspiring his people to fight to the death. But if this were the reason for Nennius' calling him *dux bellorum*, what about the incidental details in the historian's account? Neither the mention of his going into battle with an image of the Virgin Mary on his shoulder nor the feat of killing nine hundred sixty men singlehanded is easy to accept literally. But it could be that when Nennius wrote, he had before him an old text that he misread. To this day, the Welsh word for "shoulder," *ysgwydd*, is almost identical with the word meaning "shield," *ysgwyd*, and it is not difficult to suppose that the Celtic words should have been similar also, if not identical. It certainly seems more probable that Arthur would have gone into battle bearing a shield on which was some badge proclaiming his faith in the Blessed Mother.

As for the remarkably large number of victims slain by Arthur at Mount Badon, the distinction might be simply that Arthur and his men were fighting this battle, not in conjunction with other British leaders, but alone against the Saxons and that Nennius probably was describing an overwhelming defeat inflicted by Arthur's cavalry alone.

It also is possible, as another writer has suggested, that Nennius was following an early Welsh poem that listed Arthur's battles and that the curiously precise number *nine hundred sixty* would become, in Welsh, "three hundreds and three twenties," an appropriate figure for a hero whose strength already was legendary in a poetry whose early forms were obsessed with the number *three*.

The next references to a historical Arthur occur in the Latin lists of events and the years in which they took place

The nine forts of the Saxon shore, bases for the Roman defense of Britain against Germanic invaders, are pictured in a medieval transcript of a fifth-century military handbook. The book organized Britain into three military commands, one of which scholars think Arthur may have inherited.

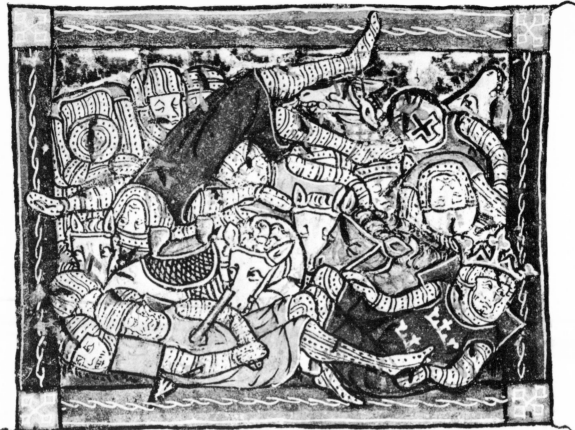

The battle of Camlann occurred, according to the Annales Cambriae, *in 537. This rendering, made some eight centuries later, powerfully conveys the bloody tangle of men and horses in which Mordred (left) and Arthur (right foreground) were fatally wounded.*

called the *Annales Cambriae.* These probably were compiled in the north of Britain about the middle of the tenth century, but they are derived from sources at least as early as those used by Nennius. These "annals of Wales," which cover the years 453 to 954, mention only the last of Arthur's battles as named by Nennius, under the date 516: "The battle of Badon in which Arthur carried the cross of Our Lord Jesus Christ, for three days and three nights on his shoulders, and the Britons were victorious." (Here again, the reference to Arthur carrying the cross on his shoulders may reflect a Welsh confusion between shoulders and shields.) Under the date 537 there is a second reference to Arthur, this time to the battle fought between him and his illegitimate son Mordred that forms the climax of the *Morte d'Arthur:* "The battle of Camlann in which Arthur and Medraut were slain; and there was death in England."

Nowhere yet is there any suggestion that Arthur was a king. But his name, which in its Latin form is Artorius,

88

suggests that he may have been of distinguished birth and from a family in some way connected with Rome. More than one Roman named Artorius lived in Britain during the empire's heyday, and one, Lucius Artorius Castus, led the sixth legion on an expedition to Armorica in the middle of the second century. It has been conjectured that an ancestor of the British Arthur may have served under him and that, proud of this service, he gave his son his leader's name, which thereafter was handed down in his family from generation to generation. But such a conjecture is not really necessary. The name Artorius implies that Arthur was of Roman descent, and the fact that he succeeded Ambrosius as leader implies that Arthur may well have been a relation of Ambrosius. According to Geoffrey of Monmouth, Ambrosius was Uther Pendragon's brother and therefore Arthur's uncle—although Uther is probably a figment of Geoffrey's lively imagination and no earlier chronicle supports this claim to royal birth. Another possibility is that after his triumph over the Saxons Arthur's men might have named their leader king, following the example of the Roman legions in fourth-century Britain who proclaimed their general, Maximus, emperor.

It is not until the late eleventh century that Arthur appears regularly and unequivocally as a king. He does so in several lives of Celtic priests and monks upon whom the Welsh and Britons somewhat freely bestowed the title of saint. In more than one of the lives, however, Arthur is called a tyrant king, and presented as a ruffianly ruler with little respect for the church, or as a *rex rebellus*, who remains

At right, Arthur sets a boatload of babies adrift on the sea—an unpleasant tale that may have originated in the Celtic monks' image of Arthur as a tyrant king. To prevent fulfillment of a prophecy that a boy born on May Day would kill him, Arthur arranged the death of all male children born that day; however, Mordred survived and later slew his father.

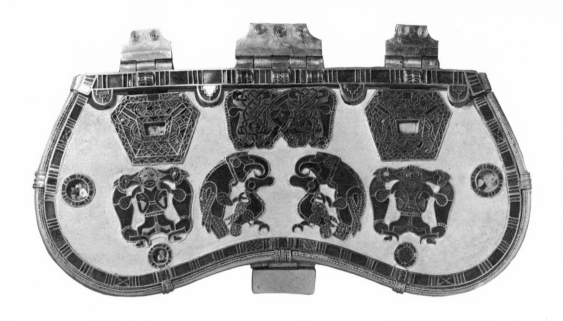

The Saxon jewelry on this page was part of a treasure unearthed at Sutton Hoo in Suffolk in eastern England in 1939. Scholars believe that a ship filled with treasure was buried there around 625 as a memorial to a wealthy Saxon. Above is a purse lid, set with garnets and colored glass depicting birds, men, and lions. Below are an exquisite clasp made of gold inlaid with glass (left) and a buckle.

evil until converted by some miracle worked by the saint whose holy career is presented for the reader's admiration and improvement. Although few of these tales about King Arthur are remotely credible, they do at least show that the monks who wrote them realized that any connection with him, however strange or fanciful, would lend credit and renown to their own, now forgotten, saintly heroes. Their less than attractive presentation of Arthur also may provide a clue to a mysterious omission in the earliest surviving chronicle of the period in which we believe him to have lived—the inference being that Arthur had in some way offended the Church in his fight for Britain's freedom.

This chronicle, *De Excidio et Conquestu Britanniae*, is the work of a sixth-century monk named Gildas. He probably was writing only a few years after Arthur's death—he may even have known Arthur. Yet he never once mentions his name.

Gildas was the son of a minor British chieftain whose small domain in Scotland was overrun constantly by Pictish marauders. He and most of his several brothers abandoned their homeland and emigrated to Wales, where they sought and were given the protection of King Caedwalla of Gwynedd. Gildas married in Wales, but his wife died young and he turned to a religious life. At various times in his career he seems to have lived in Ireland, on a lonely island in the Bristol Channel—where he lived as a hermit on fish and gulls' eggs—in Brittany, and at Glastonbury in Somerset. On his death he was deemed worthy to be considered a saint.

His main work, the *De Excidio et Conquestu Britanniae*, was written in about 540. He himself refers to it as a *liber querulus*, a book of complaints. It castigates his contemporaries for their lack of foresight and for their blindness to the lessons of the past; it attacks the local kings of Britain for immorality and tyranny. "They have many wives, and all of them adulteresses and prostitutes. They often take oaths, and always break them. They wage wars, and the wars are unjust on their own countrymen. They hunt down thieves in the countryside, but they have thieves at their own tables, whom they love and load with gifts. . . ."

Gildas briefly summarizes the historical events that led up to this appalling state of affairs. He ends with a great victory over the Saxons in a battle that he says was fought in the year of his birth, that is, in about 500; and this victory put an end to foreign wars, though not to civil wars. The name of this decisive victory is the siege of Mount

This sword handle, made of horn and decorated with pieces of metal, was used by a Saxon in the seventh century; contemporary Britons also used heavy iron swords that were elaborately decorated.

Badon—the last of the twelve victories attributed to Arthur by Nennius, and the famous battle in which, so the *Annales Cambriae* record, Arthur carried the cross of Christ for three days and three nights. But Gildas says nothing of Arthur, to whom the later chronicles give credit for the victory, referring merely and very briefly to the battle at which there was no small slaughter of those "gallows-birds," the Saxons.

This strange omission led some later historians to believe that there was no such man as Arthur. Some suggested that the whole Arthurian epic was a fabrication, a characteristic result of wishful thinking at a time when a national hero was desperately needed, or an attribution to one man of the virtues and achievements of a score of lesser men who fought against the powers of darkness. It was true, went the argument, that Gildas did not mention many names in his text; but the name of Ambrosius was given. Why not the name of Arthur, then, if it really was Arthur who had won a victory so complete that Britain had been granted peace for almost half a century?

The question has at least two answers, both of which are credible. One could be that Gildas may have had some good reason for not naming Arthur directly and that instead he mentioned him in an oblique way that his contemporaries would have understood, although we do not.

Gildas refers in his attacks on the wicked rulers of his time to one Welsh king, Cuneglasus, who was a "despiser of God, an adulterer, and an oppressor of monks." Yet in the better days of his youth Cuneglasus had driven "the chariot which carried The Bear." Who was this great man, known as The Bear, who should have a prince of royal blood to drive his chariot? Gildas does not say. But the Celtic word for "bear" is *arth* or *artos*.

There also is the possibility that Gildas did not mention Arthur by name because Arthur, like so many of his contemporaries, had fallen short of the monk's strict ideals in religion and morals and that Gildas had quarreled with him.

Arthur might also, like Cuneglasus, have been considered an "oppressor of monks." Fighting the Saxons was a costly enterprise, and a war leader who ranged as far as Arthur presumably did must have had occasion often to call upon monasteries for help in providing money and food for his men and fodder for his horses. Frequently he must have been forced to seize what was not given freely. Such high-handed impositions certainly could account for the unsympathetic figure Arthur cuts in the later saints' lives that already have been mentioned.

The primitive memorial above honors Voteporius, a Welsh chieftain whom Gildas sourly dismissed as a murderer and adulterer. The chieftain probably was Arthur's contemporary; his great-grandson, we know, was named Arthur.

PROFESSOR LESLIE ALCOCK,
UNIVERSITY COLLEGE, CARDIFF

In a scene from a miniature decorating Gildas' life of St. Eustace, the querulous monk is portrayed at left, raising an appropriately admonishing finger at a youth with a book in his hand who probably is one of Gildas' pupils.

But there may have been something more personal in the quarrel—if quarrel indeed there was—between Gildas and Arthur. According to a biography of Gildas, written in the twelfth century in Llancarfan Abbey, where Gildas himself had once lived, Arthur had killed Hueil, Gildas' eldest brother. Hueil had not gone to Wales, like the rest of his family, but had remained in Scotland to inherit his father's lands. He had come, it seems, to some traitorous understanding with the Picts in order to secure possession of his kingdom. Thus Arthur made war on him. Hueil was defeated and slain, and Gildas, who had in the past "diligently loved Arthur," now turned against him as the cause of his beloved brother's death. A similar story also appears in another eleventh-century Welsh tale, which indicates at least that Gildas' biographer did not invent the story of the quarrel. If there is any truth in the story, if Gildas and Arthur did find themselves on opposite sides in the civil wars that followed the battle of Mount Badon and that led to the fight between Arthur and Mordred at Camlann, then Gildas' reluctance to mention his brother's destroyer is explained. He could scarcely deny the triumph of Mount Badon, but he could not bring himself to record the name

A French Arthurian romance, completed about 1390 when the legend was at its most popular, contains this colorful scene of Arthur and King Ban planning a tourney. The kings converse animatedly against a background of solid gold, while Guinevere stands behind Arthur (right) with a pet dog in her arms and one of Ban's followers carries the king's falcon (left). Above the Gothic arches a centaur, half man, half horse, waves his sword.

of the victor. There is also a long-standing tradition that Gildas did, in fact, write about Arthur but later threw the book that included his name into the sea.

In the end, though, it may not even be necessary to find farfetched reasons for the fact that Arthur's name does not appear in the *De Excidio*. If the battle of Mount Badon was as resounding a victory as all accounts suggest that it was, its details would be perfectly well known to all the book's readers. Gildas had no need to repeat the information that Arthur had won it—it would have been a fact of life, taken for granted by everyone.

Certainly, by the time Nennius was writing, two hundred fifty years later, Arthur had been accepted as the victor at Mount Badon and as the paragon of British heroes. Not only in Britain was this so, but also in Brittany, where so many Britons had fled after the Saxon invasions. They took with them stirring stories of the mighty warrior, marvelous tales that later were embellished and adapted to the taste of the people in whose land they settled. But the basic material remained surprisingly close to the Celtic legends and poems of Wales and the British West Country, where Arthur's great deeds were treasured and his praises sung. The common people, the descendants of the Britons Arthur had fought to defend, never lost faith in the leader who had been their champion. Indeed, over the years their belief became still more fervent.

If you do not believe me [wrote a twelfth-century French theologian], go to the realm of Armorica [to Brittany] which is lesser Britain, and preach about the market places and villages that Arthur the Briton is dead as other men are dead, and facts themselves will show you how true is Merlin's prophecy, which says that the ending of Arthur shall be doubtful. Hardly will you escape unscathed, without being overwhelmed by the curses or crushed by the stones of your hearers.

By the twelfth century, as we have seen, Arthur's fame had spread far beyond Britain and Brittany—to France, to Germany, and to Italy. The sixth-century British warrior whose true self long since had been obscured by the mists of time had become one of the most celebrated heroes of Christendom. To the peasant he was the just protector, who one day would rise again to right their wrongs; to his lord Arthur was the model of knightly virtue; to all men Arthur's courage offered hope, and his prowess inspiration. Naturally, proof of his existence was sought—yet proof, beyond the brief mentions in the chronicles, was strangely

Arthur's decision to fight the pagan Saxons with an image of the Virgin on his shield is echoed in this fourteenth-century illustration, in which an armed knight carries the Virgin's picture on both his shield and his standard.

For centuries legend has associated the marshy, mysterious country around Glastonbury in Somerset with the island of Avalon, where Arthur was taken to be healed of his wounds. This view from a bridge once known as the Bridge Perilous shows the peaceful waters of the River Brue, which local tradition names as the last resting place of Arthur's sword, Excalibur.

Weekend Telegraph, LONDON

lacking. Then, in 1191, the skeptics suddenly were confounded by a remarkable discovery, which seemed to establish Arthur once and for all as an actual historical figure.

This discovery was made in the heart of the West Country—Arthur's traditional realm—at Glastonbury in Somerset, known in local lore as the Isle of Avalon, to which Arthur was borne, after the fateful battle of Camlann, for the healing of his grievous wound.

Once Glastonbury was, indeed, an island. In earlier times the waters of the Bristol Channel had reached deep into the Somerset levels, covering great stretches with shallow tidal water, amid which the present hills and ridges stood up like islands. In the midst of this expanse, at Glastonbury, the Iron Age British of the second century B.C. built themselves villages of timber huts on patches of dry land and fortified them against wild animals and other marauders. The so-called lake village at Glastonbury rested on timber platforms, supported by massive posts driven into the marsh and peat.

The people who lived here, in circular huts of wood and clay with roofs of reed thatch, were far from being a barbarous community. They were skillful farmers who grew wheat and barley, peas and beans; they were expert carpenters, wood carvers, and basket makers; they were expert, too, in metalwork and pottery, even in glasswork. Although they were under steadily increasing pressure from Belgic warrior tribes, who had crossed over from northeastern Gaul to settle in Britain, they managed to maintain this astonishingly high standard of civilization for more than a century. Then, shortly before the first Romans landed in Britain, in 55 B.C., the village was attacked by a powerful force of Belgic raiders, all its buildings were destroyed, and most of its people were massacred.

The peace that Roman power brought to Britain enabled the survivors of the massacre to move away to drier and more healthy ground, and Glastonbury probably became once more the deserted swamp it had been before the lake village was built. Over the centuries, however, there were changes in sea level that had the effect of partially draining the marsh, and at some period in early Christian times—no one knows when, but it certainly was well before the end of the sixth century—a monastery was built there. Its monks used to claim that the Glastonbury monastery was the oldest such foundation in Britain, and the supposed original abbey church, the Vetusta Ecclesia, a primitive construction of wattle and daub, was reverently shown to the crowds of pilgrims who flocked to Glastonbury to see "the source and fountain of all religion" in Britain.

It certainly was shown to William of Malmesbury, the most reliable of all twelfth-century historians, when he visited Glastonbury at some date between 1125 and 1135. He seems to have entertained some doubts about its age and authenticity, but he was sufficiently impressed by the abbey's ancient documents to put on record his opinion that the Church of St. Mary at Glastonbury was indeed "the first church in the kingdom of Britain."

Delighted to have confirmation of their most ancient foundation from so respected an authority as William of Malmesbury, the monks at Glastonbury made and circulated several copies of his *De Antiquitate Glastoniensis Ecclesiae*. Indeed, they went further than this: they issued new and altered editions of the work, leaving William's name on the title page but adding new material to the abbey's greater credit. Included was an account of how the abbey definitely had been founded by "no other hands than those of the disciples of Christ," who had come to England in A.D. 63 to preach the Gospel. The group was led by Joseph of Arimathea, the follower of Jesus who had begged Christ's body from Pilate and laid it to rest in the sepulcher. A British king, impressed by their conduct, gave them land on which to settle at Glastonbury. There they were visited by the Archangel Gabriel, who told them to build a church of boughs, the original of the Vetusta Ecclesia, to be dedicated to the Virgin Mary.

Gradually, as new editions of William's book were issued by succeeding generations of monks, each copy written and illuminated with infinite care and artistry, further details were added. St. Joseph of Arimathea had brought with him to Glastonbury, if not the Holy Grail itself, at least a

Set in the quaintly decorated border of a fourteenth-century English psalter is a tiny scene reminiscent of the Somerset legend in which an angelic vision instructed Joseph of Arimathea and his disciples to settle and build a church at Glastonbury.

pair of stoppered vessels, one containing the blood, the other the sweat of Christ, and these two vessels had been buried with him in the abbey grounds. At the foot of Glastonbury Tor, the hill that rises so steeply above the abbey, St. Joseph had knelt to pray, leaning on his staff as he did so, and the staff immediately had taken root and budded. This was the origin of the celebrated Glastonbury Thorn, which flowered every year at Christmas and continued to do so until a Puritan cut it down and burned it in the seventeenth century. (It did not die out altogether, however, for cuttings taken from it have continued to the present day to bloom within a week of Christmas.) Most important of all for our story, although William of Malmesbury himself never had linked the name of Arthur with Glastonbury, it eventually appeared from later versions of his book that the king, a benefactor and patron of the abbey, actually was buried there, in the grounds that once had been known as the Isle of Avalon.

William certainly had mentioned Arthur in another work, his great history of England, *De Gestis Regum Anglorum*, in which he wrote of him as a man "truly worthy to be celebrated . . . . since for a long time he sustained the declining fortunes of his country, and incited the unbroken spirit of the people to war. Finally, at the battle of Mount Badon, relying upon the image of the Mother of the Lord which he had fixed upon his armour, he made heed single-handed against nine hundred of the enemy and routed them with incredible slaughter." But William had taken pains to separate the real Arthur from the fanciful figure of Celtic legend and romance—those "foolish dreams of deceitful fables," as he called them—and he went on to state that "the grave of Arthur is nowhere known."

The Glastonbury monks, however, cast such caution aside. Geoffrey of Monmouth's *History of the Kings of Britain* had been completed in 1139, within a few years of William of Malmesbury's visit to Glastonbury, and had made the name of King Arthur revered throughout most of the Christian world. Who could blame them for giving authority to the local tradition that Arthur had been laid to rest at Glastonbury? And what Englishman could not feel gratified when, in 1191, it appeared that their faith had been rewarded at last by proof?

The story of the monks' discovery began on May 25, 1184, when a fierce fire broke out in the abbey, destroying nearly all its buildings and its precious relics, including the old church. The tragedy was complete; but the monks were

TEXT CONTINUED ON PAGE 102

GALAHAD: THE QUEST FOR THE GRAIL

The Grail was introduced into the Arthurian legend by Chrétien de Troyes in the twelfth century. In his romance, Percival, visiting a king's castle, saw the figures at left, the damsel carrying a covered Grail containing the Eucharistic wafer. In later versions of the story the Grail became the chalice containing the blood of Christ crucified, and Galahad, Lancelot's son, was the knight chosen to achieve it through his purity. At right, Galahad, with an angel on his helmet, fights the Seven Deadly Sins in order to rescue the Seven Virtues. In the Victorian tapestry below, woven by William Morris' factory to a design by Edward Burne-Jones, Galahad adores the Holy Grail while Lancelot and a kneeling Bors watch from a distance.

TEXT CONTINUED FROM PAGE 99

resourceful men. Encouraged by King Henry II, who agreed to contribute a substantial sum for the rebuilding of the abbey, they set about the task of raising money themselves. They went out into the country to beg; they solicited subscriptions from wealthy nobles; they recovered as many as they could of the relics that had been burned and exhibited them in shrines where pilgrims could bring their offerings. They managed to find the remains of several saints, including the bones of St. Patrick, the apostle of Ireland, and a skeleton that they claimed to be that of St. Dunstan, a former abbot of Glastonbury and Archbishop of Canterbury—a claim that aroused much indignation at Canterbury, where the monks had been showing St. Dunstan's tomb to pilgrims for over two hundred years.

The Glastonbury monks collected enough money to begin making plans for rebuilding on a most lavish scale; and by 1186, the first stage of the work was completed with the dedication of a new Lady Chapel. But in 1189 Henry II died, and his successor, Richard I, had no money to spare to rebuild abbeys in England while there were Saracens to fight in the Holy Land. Apparently the idea already had been formed of a search for King Arthur's tomb. The monks now went to work in earnest—and it was nothing less than Arthur's grave that in 1191 they claimed to have discovered.

The story of the discovery is related by Giraldus Cambrensis (Gerald of Wales), a contemporary historian who visited the abbey soon afterward' and met the abbot. Giraldus may be considered a reliable authority, for he refused to accept the truth of much of the Arthurian legend and condemned Geoffrey of Monmouth for propagating the fancies that had appeared in the *History of the Kings of Britain.*

According to Giraldus, the monks at Glastonbury were given an indication of where to search by Henry II himself, who had been told by "an ancient Welsh bard, a singer of the past, that they would find the body at least sixteen feet beneath the earth, not in a tomb of stone, but in a hollow oak." It had been buried at such a depth "that it might not by any means be discovered by the Saxons, who occupied

One of a monastery's most important tasks was the copying of manuscripts in its library, or as at Glastonbury, the bringing out of new editions. In the scriptorium, or writing room, monks specially skilled in calligraphy and illumination would work for hours on end, like the two copyists laboring at right in a German monastery of the eleventh century.

Going on pilgrimage was a major diversion in the Middle Ages; it coupled a chance to travel with an opportunity to beg a saint's intercession with God. Devout folk often traveled great distances to visit famous centers like Glastonbury or Canterbury, the destination of the group in the illustration above.

the island after his death, whom he had so often in his life defeated and almost utterly destroyed."

The monks roped off an area in the abbey grounds, erected a screen around it, and began to dig. They had gone but a foot or two when a spade struck against a slab of stone. Beneath the stone was a lead cross, and on the side of the cross that faced the stone were letters roughly incised.

The letters spelled out this legend in Latin:

HIC IACET SEPULTUS INCLYTUS REX ARTHURUS CUM WEN-
NEVERIA UXORE SUA SECUNDA IN INSULA AVALLONIA
Here lies buried the renowned King Arthur with Guinevere his
second wife in the Isle of Avalon

Excavating farther in growing excitement, the monks hit upon a length of hard wood. They pushed the soil away to reveal a vast coffin fashioned from a hollow oak trunk; and bursting open the lid with an iron bar, they found inside a collection of bones, the bones of an enormously tall and strong man at one end of the coffin and those of a woman at the other. The skull of the woman still was encircled by "a yellow tress of hair still retaining its colour and its freshness"; but when a monk eagerly reached down to touch the hairs, they crumbled into dust at the touch of his fingers and he himself lost his balance and fell into the grave, covering himself with mud and clay.

The bones of the man were recovered less clumsily; and as each one appeared, the monks marveled at the size of them. His shin bone, Giraldus concludes his account, "when placed against that of the tallest man in the place, and planted in the earth near his foot, reached, as the Abbot showed us, a good three inches above his knee. And the skull was so large and capacious as to be a portent or a prodigy, for the eye-socket was a good palm in width. Moreover, there were ten wounds or more, all of which were scarred over, save one larger than the rest, which had made a great hole."

Arthur and Guinevere had been found at last! Now Glastonbury Abbey could be sure of throng upon throng of visitors and pilgrims bearing gifts throughout the ensuing years. Slowly the new buildings rose toward the sky, replacing those destroyed in the recent fire; a church that eventually would be the largest in England took its splendid shape—the sprawling ruins of this beautiful abbey may be seen still. And in 1278, on the occasion of a visit to Glastonbury by King Edward I and Queen Eleanor, the remains of Arthur and Guinevere were moved reverently to a black marble tomb in the center of the choir and there laid to rest. Two stone lions were placed at each end of the tomb, a statue of King Arthur at the foot, and the leaden cross found in the original tomb was placed above it, to indicate to the pilgrims of succeeding centuries where Britain's hero lay.

The tomb remained undisturbed until the sixteenth century, when Henry VIII proclaimed the dissolution of all

While on a visit to Glastonbury, the Elizabethan antiquary William Camden made this drawing of the cross found in Arthur's grave; it is our only depiction of the cross, which has since disappeared. Note that the inscription as given here differs from that reported by Giraldus Cambrensis.

Britain's monasteries. The abbey's lands passed into private hands, and the buildings were allowed to fall into ruins. In time both the shrine and the original site of Arthur's grave were lost; and in the eighteenth century the lead cross, too, disappeared. The story of the monks' remarkable discovery came to be derided as a typical medieval fraud.

Certainly the lead cross was not a sixth-century one. A drawing made of it by a seventeenth-century historian who had seen it shows a script of a much later date. In addition, the reference to Arthur as king indicates that it was made long after his death at a time when his kingship had become part of the legend. It is impossible to be certain about the bones; they may have been those of a gigantic Iron Age warrior and his woman, buried in a dugout canoe from the Glastonbury lake village after its destruction by the Belgae. The monks may have found them by chance while digging

The ruins of Glastonbury Abbey that have survived into our own day indicate its former magnificence. The plaque visible in the center of the photograph, beneath the pillars that used to support the abbey's tower, marks the spot where Arthur's shrine once stood.

Weekend Telegraph, LONDON

a grave; or they could have found them elsewhere and placed them in the spot most convenient for their discovery.

In addition, the Abbot of Glastonbury and his monks were not alone in wanting to make the discovery of Arthur's tomb; King Henry II also was interested, although he himself died before it actually was found. Potential trouble was stirring in Wales, whose people were in a constant state of rebellion. The legends of Arthur's survival were known to all Welshmen: there was real danger that a rebel leader might arouse widespread support by declaring that he was Arthur risen again to lead them against their Norman oppressors. It would be a wise precaution to offer proof to these descendants of the Britons that Arthur really was dead.

Yet in recent years the monks' story has been shown not to be a complete fabrication. In 1934 an archaeological team digging in the abbey ruins came across the base of King Arthur's shrine; and in 1962 another team identified the site of a grave that must be the one the monks claimed to have dug up. It is possible that it was indeed Arthur's grave, and that it originally had been marked as such by the stone slab that the monks discovered, but that over the years the stone had been covered over by earth and the site lost to view. The cross could have been placed beneath the stone when the grave was marked as Arthur's, say, in the tenth century, when St. Dunstan was Abbot. Experts contend that its lettering could have been done then, and certainly the placing of lead crosses in graves was a common tenth-century practice.

There is also the fact that the other Glastonbury claims were quickly discredited, as Geoffrey Ashe, a well-known writer on the Arthurian legend, has pointed out:

The bones of St. Patrick and St. Dunstan were denounced as spurious by indignant voices from Ireland and Canterbury. But the Welsh made no comment on the depressing exhumation of their national chief. They offered no alternative legend, they produced no counter-Avalon [indeed, no place in Britain other than Glastonbury ever has claimed to be the Isle of Avalon], such an acquiescent hush has its own eloquence. It hints at a long-standing tradition of Arthur's death and interment in the monastery, not widely familiar, but so fully accepted . . . that once the secret was out the English assertions could not be denied.

In any case, the 1962 discovery of the site of the grave, whether Arthur's or not, was the first of a series of archaeological finds that now are combining to suggest that much more of the Arthurian legend may rest on fact than ever before has been supposed.

GLASTONBURY EXCAVATION COMMITTEE

This ornate twelfth-century capital once decorated Glastonbury's cloisters. After the disastrous fire of 1184 the abbey had to be almost totally rebuilt, and fragments like this capital are all that survive from the earlier foundation.

V

THE QUEST FOR CAMELOT

The discovery in 1962 of the apparent site of Arthur's grave at Glastonbury led to renewed interest in the whole of that area of Somerset, and in particular, in the persistent legend that the hill known as South Cadbury Castle, twelve miles southeast of Glastonbury, was once the famous Camelot, site of King Arthur's court.

In the early sixteenth century the antiquarian John Leland visited the sleepy little village of South Cadbury while touring England to gather information for his great work on the "History and Antiquities of this Nation." Their hill, the villagers told him, was "Camallate, sumtyme a famose toun or castelle"; they had heard "say that Arture much resortid to Camalat." The top of the hill, where the circling ramparts of a centuries-old British hill fort could be traced beneath the grass, was known as Arthur's Palace, or so another antiquarian, William Camden, recorded when he visited Cadbury in Queen Elizabeth's day. Within less than an hour's walk were two villages named Queen's Camel and West Camel. On the banks of the Cam, a stream that wound through them, a great battle had been fought— the battle of Camlann, where Mordred had been slain and from which Arthur, grievously wounded, had been carried away to the Isle of Avalon at Glastonbury, only a few miles to the north across the low-lying Somerset basin.

These local traditions have long aroused the curiosity of antiquaries and archaeologists because they have an undeniable air of authenticity. The villages of Queen's Camel and West Camel are as real as South Cadbury itself; King Arthur's Causeway, which used to run across the marsh beneath the ramparts of the hill fort, can be traced in parts along the now well-drained fields of the surrounding farms.

The grassy ramparts of South Cadbury Castle, legendary site of Camelot, are pierced by the trenches of excavators seeking signs of its occupation in the sixth century. The bronze A, found during the digging, is probably Roman.

Gloucester

WALES

COTSWOLD HILLS

BADBURY HILL

Severn

Swindon

Bristol

MARLBOROUGH DOWNS

Baydon

Dinas Powys △

Bath

Bedwyn

Kennet

Thames

WANSDYKE

WANSDYKE

INKPEN

BRISTOL CHANNEL

MENDIP HILLS

SAVERNAKE FOREST

△ Brent Knoll

Wells

QUANTOCK HILLS

△ Glastonbury

Salisbury

Winchester

Parrett

South Cadbury

Yeo

West Camel

Southampton

BADBURY RINGS

Stour

Selsey

SELSEY BILL

ISLE OF WIGHT

N

ENGLISH CHANNEL

West Camel

Cam

South Cadbury

Cale

Yeo

Queen's Camel

Stour

0   10   20
Scale of Miles

This map of the southwestern portion of England shows the various places associated with Arthur in this book. The suggested line of lookouts linking South Cadbury with Dinas Powys in Wales can be seen at upper left; inset is a detailed map of the Cadbury area.

The Cam still winds through the fields between them, and at the foot of the hill hurried burials did take place in the distant past, indicating that a battle had been fought there. Over the centuries ploughshares turning up the ground of the eighteen-acre field atop the summit uncovered a remarkable assortment of Roman coins, pottery, slingstones, building materials, and even traces of walls. It seemed that the hill, which had been occupied by Neolithic men more than three thousand years before the birth of Christ, still was inhabited at the time of the original Roman occupation of Britain. What the archaeologists and antiquarians did not know, however, was whether there ever had been an extensive reoccupation of the fort in the late fifth or early sixth century, the period in which Arthur must have lived.

When, in the 1890's, a party of antiquarians appeared on the hill to search for evidence of such a reoccupation, an old man came up to them and anxiously asked if they had come to take away the sleeping king from the hollow hill. What was found on that occasion is not recorded, but when a more scientific excavation was carried out shortly before World War I, several fragments of Romano-British pottery were uncovered, together with pieces of late Celtic workmanship. This was scarcely enough to establish a connection between South Cadbury Castle and Camelot.

In the 1950's, however, further discoveries were made, including pottery that dated from the Neolithic period and from the pre-Roman Iron Age. Most interesting of all from the Arthurian point of view, there also were pottery fragments that were similar to some already unearthed at the Early Christian monastery at Tintagel in Cornwall, as well as other shards of what may be a Merovingian glass bowl of a type imported from the Continent in the sixth century.

These important discoveries were identified by Dr. Ralegh Radford, a well-known Devonshire archaeologist, expert on Early Christian archaeology, and the most recent excavator of Glastonbury Abbey. Here was confirmation at last, Dr. Radford felt, "of the traditional identification of the site as the Camelot of Arthurian legend." Another whose interest was aroused was Geoffrey Ashe, author of a number of articles and books on the Arthurian period and legend. But without large sums of money, no proper excavation of the site could be undertaken, and the collection of sufficient funds to make a formal investigation of South Cadbury seemed unlikely until 1965, when Dr. Radford and Mr. Ashe finally succeeded in forming a Camelot Research Committee. The presidency of this committee was accepted by Sir Mortimer Wheeler, the world-famous excavator of Mohenjo Daro and the Indus civilizations of India, and the direction of the work was entrusted to Mr. Leslie Alcock, Reader in Archaeology at the University College of South Wales. Newspapers and book publishers, the British Broadcasting Corporation, various learned societies, universities, and many private donors all gave financial help. The excavations were not to be limited to an effort to discover Camelot; they were to be devoted to unearthing all the secrets of the hill's history from its earliest

This seven-foot-high monolith, inscribed in Latin with the words "Tristram lies here, the son of Cynvawr," stands by a roadside in Cornwall. Archaeologists believe it dates from the sixth century, the period when the Arthurian Tristram might possibly have lived.

OVERLEAF: *Although the diggers at Cadbury are seeking signs of a sixth-century reoccupation of a primitive hill fort, the popular vision of Camelot still is of a splendid, medieval city. In this fourteenth-century Italian manuscript, Arthur is blessed by a bishop in a Mediterranean-style Camelot full of color and light.*

Glastonbury Tor today is crowned with a fourteenth-century tower, last relic of a medieval monastic community atop its summit. Recent excavations there have uncovered the bronze head at left and other signs of a sixth-century occupation. One archaeologist believes the Tor was a lesser chieftain's fort, which also may have been a signaling station for Arthur's stronghold at Cadbury from which the hilltop is clearly visible.

known occupation by Neolithic man. Naturally, however, the chief interest focused upon the chances of finding actual archaeological proof of Arthur's having lived there.

These hopes were much increased by exciting finds that had been made at Glastonbury Tor, the strange, towering hill that rises so sharply above the ruins of the abbey. For here, in the early 1960's, a series of digs unearthed numerous fragments of sixth-century amphoras, imported from the Eastern Mediterranean, which once may have contained wine and oil, together with enough other clues to establish definitely that in the sixth century—Arthur's period—Glastonbury Tor must have been the site of the residence of some very important person.

Philip Rahtz, the director of excavations at Glastonbury, believes that at that time Glastonbury Tor may have been the stronghold of a local chieftain and perhaps served

as a signal station of some kind. It could have been linked with South Cadbury Castle—the legendary Camelot—to the south; with Brent Knoll, at the western end of the Mendip Hills, to the north; and from Brent Knoll still farther north across the mouth of the River Severn to another sixth-century British camp at Dinas Powys in South Wales. At least it is certain that when standing on Brent Knoll, one can see clearly both Cadbury Castle and Dinas Powys, which is a total distance of over forty miles. It also is likely that co-operation between the British on both sides of the Severn estuary was very close in the sixth century, with communications between them well co-ordinated. Not until the Battle of Dyrham in 577, some sixty years after Arthur's fight at Mount Badon, were the Saxons able to break through the line that connected the British defenders in Wales with those in the area of South Cadbury Castle.

TRISTRAM AND ISEULT: THE TRAGIC LOVERS

The romance of Tristram, nephew of King Mark of Cornwall, and Iseult, whom he escorted from Ireland to marry his uncle, is best known today through Richard Wagner's opera *Tristan und Isolde*, first produced in 1865. The tale of the doomed couple, who fall in love after drinking a magic potion, originated some thousand years earlier; the illustrations here were done between the thirteenth and fifteenth centuries. A tile from the floor of an English abbey (above) shows Tristram teaching Iseult to play the harp. In a French miniature (below, left), King Mark finds the lovers, who are sleeping innocently with a sword between them. On a German comb, above, left, Mark climbs a tree to eavesdrop on Tristram and Iseult, but they see his reflection in a pool. Two scenes are combined in the French illustration at right. In the foreground, the pair drink the love potion as they travel from Ireland to Cornwall. At top, a ship carries home the bodies of Tristram, who died from a sword wound, and his Iseult, who died of a broken heart.

TEXT CONTINUED FROM PAGE 115

Extensive digging at South Cadbury Castle began in the summer of 1966. The team of archaeologists and students who climbed the steep track to the summit of the hill, past King Arthur's Well, could not fail to hope that some astonishing discovery would be made that would establish Arthur's identity once and for all, incontrovertibly linking the hill with Camelot. On reaching the summit and looking down across the banks and ditches of the great ramparts that fall steeply away to the neat fields below, it certainly was possible to imagine, instead of those fields, the misty, haunted swamps that once were in their place and to picture Arthur riding out across the causeway to do battle against his enemies. For there is no doubt that to all but the most unimaginative minds, South Cadbury Castle is a strangely and strongly evocative place, at once both romantic and mysterious.

One young volunteer, who climbed the hill eagerly each morning from the school where she and most of the other student volunteers were lodged, said that every day she felt the same excitement; intuitively, she was convinced that here was Camelot. She felt sure that one day, as she and her friends knelt, scraping, in the trenches, or sat in the sunlight, washing the objects so carefully sieved from the soil, one day they would come across the longed-for incontrovertible proof.

But the digging that first year of 1966 revealed nothing so dramatic as a silver horseshoe or even a medallion bearing the vital, revealing legend ARTORIUS. Perhaps it was unrealistic to hope for such clues: no coins minted in Britain in the sixth century ever have been discovered anywhere. But quite a few inscriptions from this period have been found in Britain and Ireland, mostly incised on stone or metal. In Ireland and the Irish colonies in the west of Britain, these inscriptions are in Ogam, an alphabet of twenty letters, consisting of upright and sloping lines arranged in groups. In Britain there are still some memorial slabs and pillars incised in the Roman fashion, although such memorials usually occur only in consecrated Early Christian cemeteries.

No inscriptions of any kind, however, turned up at South Cadbury in 1966. But the excavations, short as they were and preliminary as they were intended to be, did reveal much that was both important and illuminating.

Among other things, they revealed an extremely thick stone wall of late Saxon date, a wall that surely must have protected a fortified *burh*, or settlement. This lent weight to

Excavators cutting through the southern ramparts at Cadbury in 1967 (opposite) wore helmets to protect them from falling stones. The deep trench revealed signs of the Saxon wall that evidently encircled the hill early in the eleventh century, when Ethelred the Unready used it as a mint. One of its coins is seen above.

PETER CLAYTON

The Observer, LONDON: CAMERA PRESS

the belief that eleventh-century coins bearing the place mark CADANBYRIG, which have been discovered elsewhere, actually were made at a mint set up at South Cadbury. The excavations also revealed pieces of Roman armor; they revealed a pre-Roman Iron Age ditch and the remains of a collapsed Iron Age house; and from the Early Christian period between Roman times and the age of the English mint they brought to light enough shards of Mediterranean wine jars and dishes to suggest some sort of occupation in the sixth century.

This brief reconnaissance [concluded the report by Leslie Alcock, the expert who conducted it], covered less than one seven-hundredth part of the interior and has amply confirmed the rich potential of South Cadbury Castle in both structural and cultural terms. Particular interest attaches to the . . . long perspective of Celtic and Romano-British occupation which forms the chronological background to the Arthurian period at Cadbury. Clearly the site, in all its aspects, now demands large-scale exploration.

Young volunteers at Cadbury took care of much of the laborious work of the excavation. The girls at right, below, use hands and tools to scrape away the soil; at rear, a group of workers examine the Stony Bank, a sixth-century rampart found beneath the regularly set stones of the Saxon wall. The same painstaking care is needed to unearth large finds or tiny ones, such as the artifacts seen in the pan in the foreground.

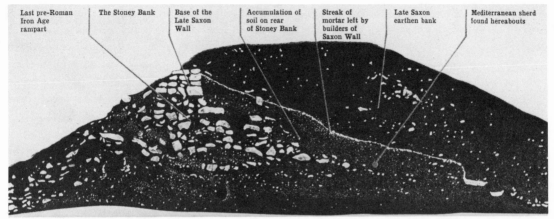

| Last pre-Roman Iron Age rampart | The Stoney Bank | Base of the Late Saxon Wall | Accumulation of soil on rear of Stoney Bank | Streak of mortar left by builders of Saxon Wall | Late Saxon earthen bank | Mediterranean sherd found hereabouts |

In the summer of 1967 excavations began again, after the Camelot Research Committee's appeal for funds had brought in further contributions from the original sponsors now joined by other newspapers, universities, and private people from all over England. That year some even more fascinating discoveries were made. For example, it definitely was established that the Saxon wall had a far more interesting history than previously had been supposed. Twenty-four feet of it was uncovered, displaying the longest stretch of Saxon wall yet seen in England. Beneath it was the last Iron Age rampart; and between the two was what the excavators called the Stony Bank.

The Stony Bank was found to contain yet another shard of imported sixth-century pottery, fragments of Roman-style roof tiles, lumps of tufa—a light stone used by the Romans in building construction—and a Roman sling-stone. The slingstone's presence showed that this layer of the wall must have been built after the Roman conquest of Britain; the tiles and lumps of tufa probably came from a pagan temple built in the third or fourth century, when there was a pagan revival in Britain, and later demolished. The remains of such temples already had been discovered in the course of excavating several other Iron Age hill forts in Britain, and the existence of such a temple naturally was expected at Cadbury. The shard of pottery presumably got there after the Stony Bank was built and certainly before the Saxon wall was erected on top of it. Thanks to these discoveries, we can infer safely that Cadbury Castle was re-fortified in the sixth century as a stronghold against the Saxon invaders. Enthusiasts have built upon this the further inference that the castle must have been occupied by the

A cross-section of the top rampart at Cadbury reveals the layers found and analyzed by researchers. At bottom are traces of the fort's occupation prior to the Roman Conquest; then comes the irregular rubble and soil of the Stony Bank, identified by the Mediterranean potshard found on top of it as sixth-century; above this bank are several courses of stones from the Saxon wall. Extensive silting caused by centuries of wind and rain has eroded the rampart, many of whose stones have fallen down.

121

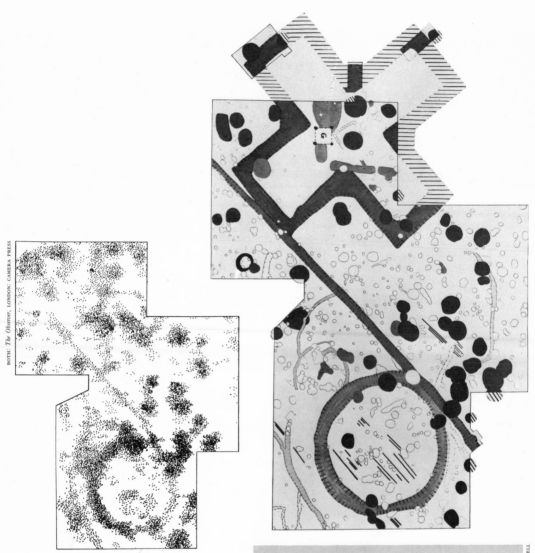

BOTH: *The Observer*, LONDON: CAMERA PRESS

MARK HOWELL

Before digging, the Cadbury excavators made a geophysical survey of the site. Using the "banjo" at right (officially called a soil conductivity meter) and other instruments that recorded differing magnetic strengths for the various underground features, they were able to plot the dot-density diagram at left above. The aerial view opposite shows the area actually laid bare for excavation, and the diagram at center indicates what was found: a ring-shaped ditch from the Iron Age, many Iron Age storage pits (dark circles), a medieval field boundary (long diagonal line), and the cruciform structure (top) that so mystified all the diggers.

type of princely warrior that Arthur is presumed to have been, but this is still supposition.

The digging out of the wall and of a new section of the summit was preceded by a geophysical survey. Instruments looking something like mine-detectors were taken over the ground to record readings that might indicate the pattern, shape, and density of the archaeological features beneath the turf. These instruments, which are known as soil conductivity meters and work on a principle similar to radar, had not been used in archaeological work before, and they were highly successful. The indications they gave of the pattern and density of postholes and storage pits enabled Leslie Alcock, the director of excavations, to decide which were

Among the finds at Cadbury was this portion of a Roman bronze shield binding, believed to date from the first-century Roman invasion of Britain. Presumably, Roman troops sacked the British hill fort, which would explain the presence of so much burned material in the Iron Age sections.

the most promising areas for that year's digging. When reduced to a printed plan, the readings revealed, by a series of dots in straight lines and in regular patterns, traces of what might have been extensive buildings constructed on top of the old Iron Age fortress in Arthur's time. One of the patterns looked remarkably like a main hall of some kind and aroused excitement among the workers.

The subsequent excavations did not reveal any more of this huge hall, but they did uncover something else of even greater interest. At first what was exposed baffled all the experts, and as the weeks of July and August, 1967, passed by, the problem seemed to grow still more incomprehensible. The diggers gradually unearthed, toward the western edge of the plot of land that had been marked out for examination, a trench that followed no explicable pattern. It zigzagged now this way and now that, until a formation something like the drawing on page 122 was discerned inside the area.

None of the experts on the site could explain what possible purpose could have been served by digging a trench in such an apparently wayward manner. At first they thought that perhaps the hill had been used for military exercises during World War I. A notice board on which the volunteer diggers were asked to suggest their own interpretations of the mystery yielded such solutions as "A giraffe's tomb," or only slightly less improbably, "Patio of King Arthur's Palace."

Then, someone studying the lines of the trench, and imagining regular patterns that would incorporate the wedge-shaped segment in the northwestern corner, suddenly realized that if the U-shaped part of the pattern were to be repeated beneath the turf outside the area of excavation, what would emerge would be a cross.

A look at the dots on the geophysical survey plan showed that the pattern did, indeed, suggest that a cruciform trench might be unearthed in that sector of the plateau. No one, however, had been looking for such a shape. The team had been seeking evidence of the round buildings that had stood there in the Iron Age and of the rectangular buildings of the Early Christian period; and traces of these they had discovered. A building in the shape of an equal-armed cross had been so far removed from any expectations of the experts that the indications of its presence had totally escaped their detection.

In excited anticipation, Mr. Alcock gave orders for three trial digs outside the excavated area. In each case the

South Cadbury's archaeological history is built upon such tiny objects as the pins, coins, and shards shown below. At right, Leslie Alcock, the excavation's director, examines some pottery fragments from the sixth century that are the basis for identifying Cadbury with Arthur's Camelot. The bowl above is made of the same fine, red pottery, called Tintagel ware, which was imported from the Mediterranean area by sixth-century Britons of wealth and position, perhaps including Arthur himself.

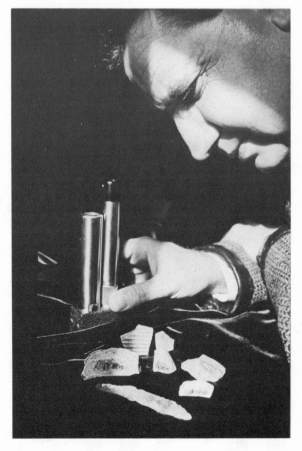

qil la uoullisent lesier en nulle menu
ere. car il ma nuls. qi ne fist paumes
et ce seroit trop grant desloiaute qi
de ce les uoulroit requerre. par soi fes
tiroie ge soi bien qe uos dites uoir.
mes la grant amors qe ge auoie auos
et as autres. les me roueues dire. Et
ne fust inchpcouenable chose ne se anz
qe le uoulisse bien. Car trop me greua
li departimenz de uos don. et des autres
spagnions
Ant ont parle entraus. qe li iors fu
biaus a esclaus alisolau. or la auqs
aluttie la rosee. et li pales. comen aen
plir des barons del roiaumes. Et la rie
qi si fu leuee. et uint la ou li rois estoit
et dit sur cil. chis. nos atanden leanz
por aler ou messe. Atant se leua li rois.
si esueuez iaus porce qe cil qe leue
ront nesachient le del qil ot mene
Et mesire. Gau comade. qe len li aport
ses armes. et ausi fist lancelot. Et qut
il sunt arme. de leur armes senz des esan
et senz des haumes. se uient el pales.
atrouutier lor spugnons qil estoient a

apareillie por aler ale glesse
Vanc il furent uenu au mostier. et
il orent oi le furise tot ici arme ai
il estoient. et il furent retorne el pales
si salerent aseoir liuns de les autre. cil
qi compignons estoient de la queste. si
re febli rois. Batemagui au roi artu.
puis qe cist afferes est empris si fiere
mat. qil ne puet mes estre leisiez. ielo
croie qe li saint fuissant aporte si si ue
ront le seiremat aussi com cil font qi
enqistre doiuent entrer. Ce le uoil bien
puis qil uos plest fet li rois. puis qil
ne puet estre. autiremat.
Des furet as clerc de leenz les sa
int aporter. sor coi en fesoit le seire
mat de la cort. et qint il furent apor
te deuat le matre dou. si apella li rois
mon seigneur. Gau. et li dit uos esme
ustes pmieremat ceste queste. Venez
auant et si ferez le seiremat qe cil
deuoient fere. qi en ceste queste uot

diggers uncovered a further section of the expected trench, so that the cruciform plan was established. By deducing the rest of the pattern from what now was known of a part of it, the foundations of an entirely logical building appeared.

This design, it was suggested at once, could be explained most easily as the plan of a church. Such a plan, in the shape of an equal-armed Greek cross, appears to have been used first in the Middle East in the late fifth century. It was by no means common, however, in Arthur's time, even in the Mediterranean area. It has been suggested that this could have been Arthur's chapel at Camelot, a chapel that later was demolished by the Saxons to provide dressed stones for part of their massive stone wall. But no traces of mortar or chips of stone have been found in the trench to lend any confirmation to this attractive hypothesis, and it seems more likely that, for some reason that we never can know, work on the building was abandoned as soon as the excavations for its foundations had been dug.

Experts now question whether the trench was dug in the sixth century, or even by the Saxons. The latest suggestion is that this unfinished foundation may have been laid as late as the eleventh century and that perhaps building was broken off when the mint was removed and the rest of the Saxon settlement was abandoned early in the reign of King Canute. So far, no firm evidence has been found to back up any of these hypotheses. And without firm evidence, the archaeologist may conjecture all he likes, but he cannot make any definite pronouncement.

Digging at South Cadbury Castle was resumed in the summer of 1968, and soon further clues were unearthed. There were several more fragments—and unusually fine fragments—of sixth-century wine jars; traces of what may well prove to be the Saxon entrance to the stronghold, the "gate of Camelot"; and part of the foundation trench for what seems to be a large, sixth-century hall cut into the bedrock of the plateau. Such a building, whose dimensions tentatively have been guessed as thirty-five feet in width and about seventy feet in length, may or may not have been the great hall of Camelot; but its discovery marks an exciting stage in the search for King Arthur's Britain, a search that still is continuing.

Identification of the cross-shaped foundations at Cadbury as those of a sixth-century church might have given an actual location to this scene, in which Arthur's knights, in the church at Camelot, swear to seek the Grail.

VI

THE ONCE AND FUTURE KING

Even if the excavations at Camelot do not eventually uncover the reality of the Once and Future King, they already have helped to dispel the illusion that Arthur was the magical king of medieval romance. We can imagine him now, not as a knightly ruler clad in gleaming armor whose natural setting is the stone halls, particolored pavilions, and painted towers of medieval Camelot, but as a stern, rough warrior face to face with the brutal facts of sixth-century warfare, living in a stronghold built for defense rather than for pleasure.

He wears, not a silver breastplate, but a leather cuirass; not a plumed helmet, but a squat, close-fitting iron headpiece lined with leather; his breeches and boots also are of leather and colored brown like his belted tunic; his trousers are of coarse linen; his red woolen cloak, the only splash of color in an otherwise drab appearance, is fastened at his right shoulder with a bronze brooch of characteristic Celtic design; at his left side hangs a heavy iron sword in a leather scabbard; in his right hand he grasps the wooden shaft of a spear whose tip is of polished iron.

With this picture of Arthur in mind, it is possible to believe that, fanciful as the legends first appeared when we came across them in the pages of Malory, in each a kernel of truth lies concealed. Undeniably, the discovery of a truth buried deep within a legend is nothing new; and in this connection the story of the German archaeologist Heinrich Schliemann is very much to the point.

As a boy in the 1830's, Heinrich Schliemann was passionately fond of fairy stories, fables, and legends. In particular, he loved the epic stories of Homer's heroes, of Achilles and Hector, Paris and Helen, and the fabulous city

In an illumination from a French manuscript of the 1300's, King Arthur rides with Lancelot, the friend who dashed all his hopes.

This splendid stone head of King Arthur, with a noble yet strangely sad expression, was carved by an unknown sculptor in the fifteenth century.

of Troy, capital of King Priam, which after a ten-year siege by the Greeks was captured, burned, and leveled. All his life Schliemann remembered that his father, a pastor from the north German state of Mecklenburg, had given him for a Christmas present when he was ten years old a book on the main events of the Trojan War and the adventures of Odysseus; that he had decided then that when he was grown up, he would go to Troy and excavate the legendary city whose whereabouts no one knew.

Schliemann left school at fourteen and worked for five and a half years in a grocery store. Then he became an office boy in Amsterdam and spent his few moments of spare time studying foreign languages, working with such diligence that he achieved fluency in English, French, Dutch, Spanish, Italian, and Portuguese. He learned Russian in order to represent his firm in St. Petersburg, and he did so brilliantly there that before long he was in business on his own account as an import-export merchant. He was incredibly successful; by 1863, he had made so much money that he was able to retire, at the age of forty-one, and devote himself to the studies that had fascinated him for so long.

An interesting feature of the Arthurian legend is the repetition by Galahad, purest of Arthur's knights, of the king's own feat of pulling a sword out of a stone. In fact, Galahad's task was the harder of the two, because his sword was in a stone that was floating in a river, as depicted here with a magically effective disregard for the laws of physics.

In 1868 he sailed for Greece, determined to prove wrong the scholars and experts who had relegated the Trojan epic to the world of myth. He was as convinced in late middle age as he had been as a boy that the Greece of Homer's *Iliad* once really had existed, that Achilles and Agamemnon, Hector and Aeneas, were actual historical heroes who had lived and fought and died. Again and again Schliemann read the *Iliad*, searching for clues that would lead him to Troy, the great city that so many scholars said never had existed, following Homer's directions as best he could. His trail led him to Hissarlik, a small town in western Turkey, a few miles from the southern entrance to the Dardanelles. There, with a millionaire's resources to indulge his whim, Schliemann set a hundred men to work digging for months on end, ignoring ridicule and discomfort alike. And there he uncovered not only the ruins of King Priam's city, but also the traces of a whole vanished civilization previously unknown to archaeology.

Schliemann's faith and ability found Troy and proved that a legend can have its base in historical reality. So may it be some day with Camelot and the facts behind the Arthurian legend. An English writer, Beram Saklatvala, recently has made several ingenious suggestions to account for some of the legend's varied details. He has guessed, for instance, that the source of the French book from which Malory claimed he had taken the story of the sword in the stone might have been a now lost Latin chronicle in which some such sentence as this occurred: "*Arthur gladium ex saxo eripuit*"—"Arthur drew, or seized, a sword from the stone." This remarkable feat, so Malory tells us, was beyond the power of other men and thus proved Arthur's right to be king. This was the kind of fantastic story that induced the printer Caxton to tell his readers that they were "at liberty to believe" that the *Morte d'Arthur* was not all true. But Saklatvala suggests, Could the Latin phrase be a mistaken copy of the record of an authentic fact?

The words that arouse disbelief are *ex saxo*, "from a stone." Medieval clerks were in the habit of omitting the letter *n* and of showing the omission by a stroke drawn in above the next letter, so that *ex saxoē*, or *ex saxone*, would mean that Arthur took the sword from the Saxon rather than from the stone, a very different and wholly credible event. Whether we are to interpret it that Arthur struck the sword from the hand of a particular and much-feared Saxon warrior in single combat, or that the Saxon is intended to mean the whole Saxon race whose ambitions were

OVERLEAF: *Arthur's knights are armed for battle by their ladies in a Victorian tapestry designed by Edward Burne-Jones and woven by William Morris. Both men were members of the Pre-Raphaelite Brotherhood, a group that sought to recreate the pure colors and the spirit of early medieval art.*

thwarted at Mount Badon, it is not difficult to believe that such a victory would ensure for Arthur the leadership of the British armies, if not indeed the throne of the surviving British kingdom in the West Country.

The story of the other sword in the legend, Excalibur, may have passed into the realm of myth by a similar process, Saklatvala believes. In Malory's version of the tale the sword appears in the midst of a lake of "fair water and broad," and after the battle of Camlann, when Arthur instructs Sir Bedivere to return it to the waters, "there came an arm above the water and met it, and caught it, and so shook it thrice and brandished, and then vanished away the hand with the sword in the water." Geoffrey of Monmouth also writes of Arthur's "peerless sword, forged in the Isle of Avalon," which he calls Caliburn.

Saklatvala suggests that there might have been an early chronicle in which Arthur was said to have obtained his sword *ex cale burno* from beside the river Cale, in which case its name and its connection with water would be readily explained. It is indeed a fact that the Romans ascribed some of the merits of their iron swords to the quality of the water into which the blacksmith plunged the heated blades in order to temper them by sudden cooling. It is also a fact that there is a river Cale within an hour's ride of South Cadbury Castle.

Unfortunately, eminent scholars have refuted Saklatvala's thesis. Apart from the fact that the medieval Latin word *burna*, "stream," is recorded for the first time only about 1135, the period in which Geoffrey actually was completing his *History*, the Somersetshire river Cale in his day was written *Cawel*, and the spelling "Cale" does not appear until Elizabethan days. There is also doubt about whether the *ex* in Excalibur stands for the Latin word meaning "out of"; it probably is just a prefix used to accentuate the first syllable in the Old French form of the word "escalibor"— an accentuation rather like that in "especial," compared with "special," for instance.

The generally accepted derivation of the name of Arthur's sword, according to the distinguished Arthurian scholar R. S. Loomis, is Celtic rather than Latin. Excalibur's name in the Welsh romances is Caledvwlch, apparently based on the Welsh words *calet*, "hard," and *bwlch*, "notch." Professor Loomis believed, however, that this was just a Welsh approximation of the name of another famous sword, renowned in Irish legends: Caladcolg, or Caladbolg, meaning "Hard Sword" or "Hard Sheath," which was made by the fairies for an Ulster hero named Fergus. In one of these Irish sagas the hero Fergus Mac Leite uses Caladcolg to do battle with a lake monster. Victorious, but mortally wounded, he begs his followers to give his sword only to another hero named Fergus and to treasure it "that none other take it from you; my share of the matter for all time shall be this: that men shall rehearse the story of the sword." There are some obvious parallels here with the story of Arthur as we know it from Malory, although no scholar has done more than point out the similarities.

The fact that the quest for Excalibur's true source leads back to Celtic myth and legend should not disappoint us unduly. It was natural that the defeated British people should glorify the memory of their greatest hero with legendary attributes that originally belonged to other heroes, or even to the gods of their pagan past. As Professor Loomis has put it:

Throughout the world's history, clouds of legend have gathered about the heads of military leaders who have caught the imagination of a people. This happened to Alexander and Charlemagne, to Napoleon and Washington. For the Britons it was enough that Arthur inflicted a series of defeats on their heathen foes and staved off for a time their expulsion from what was to be England. . . . To this racial hero the Welsh and to some extent the Cornish attached a floating mass of native traditions, together with matter derived from Ireland and the Britons of the North. This they passed on to the Bretons, who shared their passionate devotion to the memory of Arthur, and the Bretons in turn, speaking French, were able by the fire and the charm of their recitals to captivate the imagination of the non-Celtic peoples. Thus the obscure battle leader of a defeated race became the champion of all Christendom, his knights paragons of valor and chivalry, and the ladies of his court nonpareils of beauty. . . .

There is actually no need to find historical parallels in order to believe in the historicity of Arthur, nor is it necessary to identify the Round Table with the war council of Arthur's cavalry commanders in order to believe that there were such commanders. We may believe nothing else in *Le Morte d'Arthur*, but of the existence of its central figure we scarcely can be in doubt. We even may believe, as one historian has said of the Glastonbury stories, that none of the Arthurian legends bears any relation to records of facts, but the existence of those legends is in itself a very great fact.

And who can say that even now, after fourteen hundred years, some vital evidence will not be found to blow away the mists of legend and reveal in sudden clarity an unde-

Drawn in the twelfth century, the plan above represents the banquet hall of Tara, palace of the high kings of ancient Ireland. The writing indicates where guests of various professions and social classes were seated during banquets and which joints of meat were assigned to them. The figure in the middle is an attendant.

TEXT CONTINUED ON PAGE 138

GUINEVERE:
THE FAITHLESS QUEEN

Guinevere's increasing importance in the Arthurian legend parallels women's emergence, over the centuries, from an inferior role. In the early tales Guinevere is little more than Arthur's chattel, notable only for her beauty. By the twelfth century, however, she had become the heroine of a courtly love affair with Lancelot, the noblest of Arthur's knights, whose reverence for her naturally increased her status. In the miniature at top left, she sits beside Arthur at table, listening to Lancelot recounting a quest. The medieval code of honor permitted this three-way relationship; by Victorian times, such adultery was inexcusable. A Gustave Doré engraving (right) portrays a repentant Guinevere begging her husband's forgiveness. The queen's character also fascinated Dante Gabriel Rossetti, who made the compelling drawing above. In 1960 the love that caused the collapse of Arthur's ideal Round Table became the theme of a Broadway musical, *Camelot*; at left are tiny dolls made by Tony Duquette to show the costumes he designed for Guinevere and Arthur.

TEXT CONTINUED FROM PAGE 135

niable truth? In the meantime, we can draw together a tentative biography of Arthur based upon the few facts we possess and the deductions that can be made from those facts.

He was born about 475 into a well-to-do West Country family and given a Roman name, Artorius, in token of the family's traditional loyalty to the empire. As a young man in the Christian kingdom of Ambrosius, the last outpost of Roman influence in Britain, he showed powers of leadership that led to his taking over the defense of the kingdom on Ambrosius' death. He formed and trained an effective force of mobile cavalry, which fought as a reliable, disciplined unit in the traditional Roman style. He persuaded most of the British kings to accept him as their supreme war leader, a Count of Britain on the Roman model, and to appoint him commander of their local levies.

With his own cavalry and what support he could pick up on his way, he ranged far and wide over the island, attacking its heathen invaders in campaigns that took him from Chester in the west to the forests of Caledonia north of Hadrian's Wall and into the lands occupied by the East Saxons and the North Angles. He succeeded in giving his cause a Christian and Catholic flavor by invoking the protection of the Virgin Mary, yet he offended the Church by the impositions he was forced to make upon the monasteries in order to obtain the supplies he needed to carry on the fight against the pagans.

In 516 his enemies converged upon his defenses in the southwest, but at Mount Badon, somewhere near the Wansdyke, he led his cavalry triumphantly against them, inflicting such an overwhelming defeat that peace reigned for a generation. It was broken by a civil war in which Arthur and Mordred, the illegitimate son who sought to replace him, both were killed. For some twenty years, however, Arthur had been the recognized master of all those parts of Britain not occupied by the Angles and Saxons. He was proclaimed king by his troops, and he held with his knights, or companions, a kind of court that later generations were to know as Camelot.

Once again, facts and speculations merge into myth, and we are left searching for that incontestable proof that some day may solve the riddle of Malory's "great conqueror and excellent King" whose story has been written anew generation after generation. To each he has had a different aspect: to one, he is a tyrant king; to another, a mighty warrior; to yet another, a fairy ruler of a magical subter-

This bronze statue of King Arthur was designed by Dürer; it presently adorns the sarcophagus— in Innsbruck, Austria—of Maximilian I, the Holy Roman Emperor who reigned from 1493 to 1519.

HOFKIRCHE, INNSBRUCK

ranean kingdom; to Malory, he is a knightly hero, noble and tragic, and it is this image of Arthur that probably has left the most lasting impression.

Yet even while Malory wrote, the temper of the times had changed. The world he described still had its appeal, even to the aggressive monarch Henry VIII, who boasted of his descent from Arthur (through the Welsh princes to whom the Tudor family were distantly related) and enjoyed jousts, tournaments, and splendid events of all kinds. But Henry was no pattern of knightly behavior, and in the upsurge of interest in Classical literature and art and the clash between Protestant and Catholic faiths that characterized the sixteenth century, the whole idea of medieval chivalry began to seem an anachronism. It was not just that new weapons had rendered knights obsolete; the Elizabethans, practical and realistic men that they were, tended to see them in terms of Cervantes' Don Quixote, insanely tilting at windmills. The unreal world of Malory's stories was replaced by the discovery of a New World, unexplored and enchanting. Who could interest himself in the fancies of Arthur's imaginary court at Camelot when Florida and Santiago beckoned the adventurous, when men could read of Drake's circumnavigation of their own globe?

Some Elizabethans could—among them Edmund Spenser, whose *Faerie Queene*, published just before the

This oaken round table, eighteen feet in diameter, may have been built as early as the thirteenth century. It probably was painted like this during the reign of Henry VII; the Tudor rose and the Tudor colors— green and white—were reminders that the royal family claimed descent from King Arthur, who is pictured atop the table encircled by the names of some of his knights. The table still hangs in Winchester Castle, which Malory believed to be the site of Camelot.

profitable; he and his epics are known today only because a far better poet, Alexander Pope, labeled him "the everlasting Blackmore" who "sings so loudly and who sings so long."

The eighteenth century saw little interest in Arthur; it was an age of reason and of practicality. Merlin already had become a figure of fun; astrologers used his head as a sign outside their fortune-telling establishments. The popular tale of Tom Thumb made the tiny man a knight at King Arthur's court, in love with the king's daughter Princess Hunca Munca. It was not until the end of the century that a rekindled interest in the Middle Ages brought Romantic poets and painters once again to the Arthurian cycle. Early in the nineteenth century Walter Scott and Robert Southey wrote on Arthurian subjects and planned or edited new versions of Malory. By the middle of the century, medievalism was a passion, reflected in the Gothic art and architecture of Victorian England. Edward Bulwer-Lytton, William Morris and the Pre-Raphaelite Brotherhood of artists and writers, Matthew Arnold, and various lesser poets turned their attention in turn to the Arthurian theme. And in 1859 Alfred Tennyson published the first series of the *Idylls of the King*, which translated Malory's characters and their acts into a gospel for Victorian times.

Tennyson had had this project in mind for many years. He had made visits to places traditionally associated with King Arthur in the West Country, seeking material and impressions. He had read and reread the *Morte d'Arthur*, and he had some knowledge, too, of the French and Norman chronicles and of the heroic legends of Wales. His first Arthurian poem, *The Lady of Shalott*, was published in 1832, when he was only twenty-three; he already was planning fragments and themes for an epic of some kind on what he called "the greatest of all poetic subjects." But he was preoccupied by other work and uncertain of exactly what shape his epic should take. By the 1850's, he had found the ideal narrative form for what was to become his lifework: a series of long, linked parts that covered the full sequence of the story from Arthur's mysterious birth to his disappearance into the mists of Avalon.

William Holman Hunt's The Lady Of Shalott, *painted between 1886 and 1905, pays tribute to Pre-Raphaelite ideals of color and detail. The lady stands encircled by her loom and entangled in its threads after her fatal glimpse of Sir Lancelot in the mirror now "crack'd from side to side."*

This photograph of Alfred Tenny-son was made in 1869. He was fifty and had just completed a second series of Arthurian Idylls. *It was taken by Julia Cameron, a celebrated early photographer who was a friend of the poet's.*

Publication of the first four idylls in 1859 was greeted with unparalleled enthusiasm. Ten thousand copies of the work were sold within the first week, and Tennyson was offered five thousand guineas for another volume of the same length. Over the next twenty-five years he added further idylls of Arthur, his knights, and the ladies of his court, and even when the series of twelve was complete, the poet continued to work with it, altering lines to make his meaning clearer, to within a year of his death in 1892. The public was enraptured; the publishers had to contend with orders for forty thousand copies even before publication. In homes all over the English-speaking world his hauntingly beautiful verses were committed to memory.

Tennyson's King Arthur, a "blameless King" of the utmost moral rectitude, is far removed from Malory's passionate knight. In the *Idylls* there is none of the open sexuality that pervades Malory's Camelot. Just as Geoffrey of Monmouth's Arthur was called into being in Stephen's time to give a heroic British origin to the newly established Norman kingdom, Tennyson's Arthur reflects the sentiments and morality admired by the current representatives of the English monarchy, Queen Victoria and her consort, Prince Albert. The poet depicts Britain of Arthur's day not as an ideal period, but as a kind of analogy from which Victorian readers could draw parallels for their own time. He wanted to stress virtues that seemed to him excellent, idealism, chivalry, unselfish patriotism, and religious faith, and to show that even the finest and greatest ideals often go down in defeat, as Arthur's did. In the end, however, his message is one of hope, as Bedivere, despairing, calls the "true old times . . . dead,/When every morning brought a noble chance,/And every chance brought out a noble knight."

And slowly answer'd Arthur from the barge:
"The old order changeth, yielding place to new,
And God fulfils himself in many ways,
Lest one good custom should corrupt the world.
Comfort thyself: what comfort is in me?
I have lived my life, and that which I have done
May He within Himself make pure! but thou,
If thou shouldst never see my face again,
Pray for my soul. More things are wrought by prayer
Than this world dreams of. . . ."

The high idealism of Tennyson's Arthur has been seen as a direct reflection of the virtues of Prince Albert, to whom, after his premature death in 1861, Tennyson dedicated the *Idylls*: "These to His Memory—since he held them dear,/Perchance as finding there unconsciously/Some image of himself. . . ." The dedication certainly makes of the epic a public compliment to the rulers whose Poet Laureate Tennyson was; but his purpose went deeper than that. The characters are symbolic: Arthur represents the ideal soul, which struggles to fulfill itself in the world of sense (represented by marriage with Guinevere), while the Round Table stands for the soul's attempt to ennoble and control human emotions—an ideal that gradually is corrupted and eroded by the sin of Lancelot and Guinevere. But as Tennyson himself put it: "Every reader must find his own interpretation according to his ability, and according to his sympathy with the poet."

The influence of Arthurian legend upon the art and literature of the period continued unabated; even the new craft of photography was employed to make a series of illustrations of Tennyson's *Idylls*, while some of the finest artists of the day contributed their own visions of Arthur's romantic and elusive world. Musicians, too, were drawn to the story of Arthur, notably the German composer Richard Wagner, who had produced the first of his Arthurian music-dramas, *Lohengrin*, in 1850 and followed it with the famous *Tristan und Isolde* in 1865 and in 1882 with *Parsifal*, based upon the German legends of Percival and the quest for the Holy Grail. To ensure the total unity that he demanded, Wagner wrote both words and music for his great operas, and the regular performance of his works at the Bayreuth festivals and their immediate and overwhelming popularity formed yet another current in the extraordinary spread of Arthurian influences.

In our own day the concept of knighthood has been celebrated anew. T. H. White's delightful books about King Arthur, which he gathered together under the title of *The Once and Future King*, have brought the legend to life for a new generation, both by themselves and through *Camelot*, the musical and the film based upon them.

White presents the story in a fresh and vivid light, filling it with humor and magic, with lessons in hawking and boar-hunting, in archery and jousting, in history and animal lore. But he treats his material with the same loving respect with which Sir Thomas Malory treated it, and at the end of the last book White actually brings Malory himself into the story, as a page with a face expressive of youth's innocence and certainty. Arthur, tired and soon to die, tells

T. H. White, whose books about Arthur have retold the old story with humor, pathos, and zest, was a man of varied interests, including the medieval art of hunting with a trained hawk; here one is perched on White's gloved hand.

the boy what the purpose of his life has been and urges him not to fight in the final battle with Mordred on the following day but to take horse to Warwickshire, there to think of himself as a kind of vessel to carry on the idea of the Round Table and spread its message to future generations.

Put it like this [Arthur says to him]. There was a king once, called King Arthur. That is me. When he came to the throne of England, he found that all the kings and barons were fighting against each other like madmen. . . . They did a lot of bad things, because they lived by force. Now this king had an idea, and the idea was that force ought to be used, if it were used at all, on behalf of justice, not on its own account. Follow this, young boy. He thought that if he could get his barons fighting for truth, and to help weak people, and to redress wrongs, then their fighting might not be such a bad thing as once it used to be. So he gathered together all the true and kindly people that he knew, and he dressed them in armour, and he made them knights, and taught them his idea, and set them down, at a Round Table. And King Arthur loved his Table with all his heart. He was prouder of it than he was of his own dear wife, and for many years his new knights went about killing ogres, and rescuing damsels and saving poor prisoners, and trying to set the world to rights. That was the King's idea.

And that, to White, was all that really mattered. He was not concerned with the "real" Arthur; he turned history upside down to recreate a medieval knight at odds with the ways of a violent world. He despised those historians and archaeologists who were trying to track a beautiful legend to its source and thus, in his view, destroy its beauty. For him Arthur was "not a distressed Briton hopping about in a suit of woad in the fifth century," but a true knight with "an open face, with kind eyes and a reliable or faithful expression, as though he was a good learner who enjoyed being alive. . . . He had never been unjustly treated, for one thing, so he was kind to other people."

More than a thousand years separates White's King Arthur and Nennius' Commander in the Battles, but perhaps they were not such different people, after all. No one ever will know. But the quest for Arthur of Britain never can destroy the beauty of the works that his legend has inspired or the fascination of the legend itself. Since Arthur's nobility and valor first inspired the hearts of his followers, his story has dignified the human spirit. The search for the man himself has become a continuing quest for what lies hidden in the hearts of all men, and it may lead us one day to the truth about the Once and Future King.

Weekend Telegraph, LONDON

An aura of Arthur's Britain still clings to the dark-shadowed wood near Camelford in Cornwall. There, according to local legend, the battle of Camlann took place, costing King Arthur his life but ensuring his fame.

FURTHER READING

Ashe, Geoffrey, *King Arthur's Avalon*. Dutton, 1958.

———, *From Caesar to Arthur*. Collins, 1960.

———, ed., *The Quest for Arthur's Britain*. Praeger, 1968.

Barber, R. W., *Arthur of Albion*. Barnes & Noble, 1961.

Bede, *A History of the English Church and People*, translated by L. Sherley-Price. Penguin, 1968 (paperback).

Chambers, E. K., *Arthur of Britain*. October House, 1967 (paperback).

Collingwood, R. G., and Myres, J. N. L., *Roman Britain and the English Settlements*. Oxford University Press, 1961.

Loomis, R. S., *Arthurian Tradition and Chrétien de Troyes*. Columbia University Press, 1949.

———, *Wales and the Arthurian Legend*. University of Wales Press, 1956.

———, *The Development of Arthurian Romance*. Hutchinson, 1963.

———, ed., *Arthurian Literature in the Middle Ages*. Oxford University Press, 1959.

———, and Loomis, L. H., *Arthurian Legends in Medieval Art*. Modern Language Association of America, Krause Reprint Co., 1966.

Maynadier, Howard, *The Arthur of the English Poets*. Houghton Mifflin, 1907, Johnson Reprint Co., 1969.

Matthews, William, *The Ill-Framed Knight*. University of California Press, 1966.

Monmouth, Geoffrey of, *The History of the Kings of Britain*, translated by Lewis Thorpe. Penguin, 1966 (paperback).

Quennell, Marjorie, and Quennell, Charles H., *Everyday Life in Roman and Anglo-Saxon Times*. Putnam, 1960.

Saklatvala, Beram, *Arthur, Roman Britain's Last Champion*. Taplinger, 1967.

Sutcliff, Rosemary, *Sword at Sunset* (fiction). Coward, 1963.

Treharne, R. F., *The Glastonbury Legends*. Cresset Press, 1967.

Vinaver, Eugène, ed., *Works of Thomas Malory*. Oxford University Press, 1954.

ACKNOWLEDGMENTS

The Editors are particularly grateful for the assistance of Mrs. Christine Sutherland in London. In addition, they would like to thank the following individuals and organizations:

W. H. Allen Publishers, London
Mr. Geoffrey Ashe
Mrs. Susan Bakker
Bibliotheque de l'Arsenal, Paris—M. Jacques Guignard
Bibliotheque Municipale de Douai—Mme. Y. Duhamel
Bibliotheque Nationale, Paris—M. Marcel Thomas; Mme. Le Monnier
Bibliotheque Royale, Brussels—M. Martin Wittek
The Bodleian Library, Oxford
British Information Service Library—Margaret Gale
Burgerbibliothek, Berne—Dr. Steiger
City Museum and Art Gallery, Birmingham
Professor Rowland L. Collins, University of Rochester
John R. Freeman Ltd., London
Hofkirche, Innsbruck
Koniklijke Bibliothek, The Hague—Mr. de Kruyter
The Lambeth Palace Library, London
Landesmuseum, Trier
The Mansell Collection, London
Österreichische Nationalbibliothek, Vienna—Hofrat Dr. Hans Pauer
The Pall Mall Press, London
The Rylands Library, Manchester
Trustees of the British Museum, London
Universitatsbibliothek, Bonn—Dr. Beckerath

The quotation on page 135 is from *Arthurian Tradition and Chrétien de Troyes*, by Roger Sherman Loomis, published by Columbia University Press, 1949. The quotation on page 146 is from *The Once and Future King*, © 1939, 1940, and 1958 by T. H. White, reprinted by permission of G. P. Putnam's Sons.

In the French illustration below, Lancelot fights with and defeats a knight who has imprisoned Gawain.

In this fifteenth-century Italian drawing, Arthur sails off to Avalon as an arm reaches out to take Excalibur. Bedivere can be seen at left.

INDEX

Boldface indicates pages on which maps or illustrations appear

A

Achilles, 129, 131
Aedán mac Gabráin, 15
Aelle, 76
Aeneas, 131
Aetius, General, 70
Agamemnon, 131
Agincourt, Battle of, 31
Agravaine, Sir, 38, 48, 50, 51
Albert, Prince, 144–145
Alcock, Leslie, 111, 120, 123, 124, 125, **125**
Ambrosius, 70, 71, **71**, 73, 76–77, 79, 89, 138
  death of, 78, **78**
Amesbury, ruins of, 53, **54**
Aneurin, 15, 16
  Gododdin, quoted, 15
Angles, 15, 60–61, 73, 82, 138
Anglesey, Wales, 134
Anglo-Saxons, war practices of, **80–81**, 81
Anir, son of Arthur, 16, 82
Annales Cambriae, 88, 92
  quoted, 88
Argyll, prince of, 15
Aristo, 140
Armorica, 73, 89, 95
Arnold, Matthew, 143
Arthur, King, **endsheets**, **6**, 7, 8, **8**, 10, **10–11**, 16, **16**, **18**, 19, 20, **20**, 21, 22, **22–23**, 26, **48**, **49**, 94, **94**, 111, **112–113**, **128**, 129, **129**, 136, **136**, 138, **138**, **150**, **back cover**
  legends of, 11–31 *passim*; places named for in England, 12; creation of legend and myth of, 12, 15–16; Geoffrey of Monmouth's account of, 16–21;

spread of legend in Europe and Asia, 21–23, 26, 28
  legend of in *Le Morte d'Arthur* by Sir Thomas Malory, 34–56, 135; birth of, 36; claiming of throne of, 37–38; coronation of, 39, **39**; and Excalibur, 38, 42, 134–135; European campaign of, 42–43; fights giant of Mont-St.-Michel, **title page**, 8, 42–43, **43**; attack on Rome and defeat of Lucius, 42, **42**, 43, **43**; as emperor of Rome, 43; love of and marriage to Guinevere, 43, **44–45**, 46–47; and Round Table, **32–33**, 33, 46–47; and quest for the Holy Grail, **cover**, 8, 47, **47**, **126**; discovery of Lancelot and Guinevere, 48, 50, 51; orders death of Guinevere, 51; leads attack on Lancelot in France, 52–53; takes Guinevere back, 53, **137**; Mordred seizes throne of, 53; last battle (Camlann) and death of, 54–56, **54–55**, **56**, **57**, **88**
  historical role as defender of Britain, 79, **79**, 80–81, 82–83, 85–86; Nennius' account of, 86, 88, 95; battles of, 88; sources of title and Roman connection of, 88–89; relation with the Church, 89, 91–93; as tyrant king, 89, **89**, 91; Gildas' account of, 91–93, 95; historical proof of, 95, 97–99; discovery of Glastonbury grave of, 102, 104–106, **105**, **106**, 107; *1962* discovery of grave of, 109
  legend of, 129–147 *passim*; role of in defense of Britain, 131, 134; biography of, 138; effect of legend on English history and literature, 139–146 *passim*; legend of in Elizabethan England, 139–140; Victorian image of in Tennyson, 143–145; T. H. White interpretation of,

145–146
Artorius, 88–89
Ashe, Geoffrey, 111
  quoted, 107
Auxerre, 66
Avalon, Isle of, 56, 97, 99, 105, 107, 109, 134, 143

B

Badbury, Wiltshire, 82
Badbury Hill, Berkshire, 82
Badbury Rings, Dorset, 82
Ban, King, 94
Basilica, London, 61, 65
Bassas, River, 81, 82
Bath, 64, **65**, 79
Bede, the Venerable, 71, 73, 76, **76**
  History of the English Church and People, 71, 76
  quoted, 73
Bedivere, Sir, 47, 55–56, 134, 144
  and Excalibur, 56, **56**
Bedwyn, 82
Belgic tribes, 97, 106
Benwick, King of, 47, 53
Blackmore, Sir Richard, 141, 143
Bors, Sir, 47, 48, 100, **100–101**
Boudicca, Queen, 66
Breconshire, Wales, 12, 16
Brent Knoll, 115
Bristol Channel, 79, 91, 97
Britain, 15, 16–17, 19, 57, 118, 140
  map of, **67**
  legend of Arthur in, 21–23
  Roman occupation and influences in, 59, 64, **64–65**, 66, 69, 70, 76, 77, 79, 82, **82**, 97, 98, 110–111, 121, 124, 138
    pottery and silver of, **64**, 65

150

152

This bronze bowl, an example of British craftsmanship, was found in an Anglo-Saxon grave in Kent.